A DEADLY
A RACE AGAINST TIME...

An asteroid was hurtling through space directly toward Earth. There was no doubt that the end of man's home planet was near at hand. But what could be done to save mankind itself? The task of evacuating the entire population of Earth was daunting enough; and it didn't help matters that the man who discovered the asteroid, Lee Kendrick, hadn't seen fit to leave the planet himself! So now there were millions who thought it was all just a ruse. They weren't going to be fooled!

But Lee Kendrick hadn't refused to leave, he had been kidnapped—kidnapped by forces with a very sinister plan. So it was up to Jay Wales, a government man on far off Mars, to find Kendrick and bring an end to the confusion. But time was running out for Wales, and Kendrick, and the world...it was Last Call for Doomsday!

FOR A COMPLETE SECOND NOVEL, TURN TO PAGE 85

CAST OF CHARACTERS

JAY WALES
He was busy helping Earthlings acclimate to their new home on Mars, then he was ordered to find Kendrick before it was too late.

LEE KENDRICK
Lee was the brilliant astronomer who discovered not only the asteroid, but a plot to keep a lot of people from being rescued.

MARTHA KENDRICK
She was tough and loyal, and when her brother went missing she was determined to find him before leaving the planet.

JOHN FAIRLIE
Entrusted as an Evacuation Marshall; unfortunately he didn't seem to think everyone was worth saving.

SAM LANTERMAN
He was a good but misguided man, and the leader of a group of people who didn't believe their world could end.

THE BROTHERHOOD OF ATONEMENT
This odd cult believed that burning the cities of Earth would appease the gods and stop the planet's destruction.

LAST CALL FOR DOOMSDAY

By
EDMOND HAMILTON

ARMCHAIR FICTION
PO Box 4369, Medford, Oregon 97504

CHAPTER ONE

A DEEP SHUDDER shook Jay Wales. He wished now he hadn't had to come back to Earth this last time. He wanted to remember the old world of man as it had been, not as it was now in its dying hour.

"It seems impossible that it will really happen," said Hollenberg, the docket captain.

He wasn't looking at Earth. He was looking beyond it at the glittering stars.

Wales looked too. He knew where to look. He saw the faint little spark of light far across the Solar System.

A spark, a pinpoint, an insignificant ray upon the optic nerves ...that was all it was.

That...and the hand of God reaching athwart the universe.

"It'll happen," said Wales, without turning. "September 27th, 1997. Four months from now. It'll happen."

The rocket-ship was suddenly convulsed through all its vast fabric by the racking roar of brake-jets letting go. Both men exhaled and lay back in their recoil-chairs. The thundering and quivering soon ceased.

"People," said Hollenberg, then, "are wondering if it really will. Happen, I mean."

For the first time, Wales looked at him sharply. "People where?"

Hollenberg nodded toward the window. "On Earth. Every run we make, we hear it. They say..."

And here it was again, Wales thought, the rumors—the whispers—that had been coming out to Mars, stronger and more insistent each week.

There in the crowded new prefab cities on Mars, where hundreds of millions of Earth-folk were already settling into their new life, with millions more supposed to arrive each month, the rumors were always the same.

"Something's wrong, back on Earth. The Evacuation isn't going right. The ships aren't on schedule…"

Wales hadn't worried much about it, at first. He had his own job. Fitting the arriving millions into a crowded new planet, a new, hard way of life, was work enough. He was fourth in command at Resettlement Bureau, and that meant a job that never ended.

Even when the Secretary called him in to the new UN capital on Mars, he'd only expected a beef about resettlement progress. He hadn't expected what he got.

The Secretary, an ordinarily quiet, relaxed man, had been worn thin and gray and nervous by a load bigger than any man had ever carried before. He had wasted no time at all on amenities when Wales was shown in.

"You knew Kendrick personally?"

There was no need to use first names. Since five years before, there was only one Kendrick in the world who mattered.

"I knew him," Wales had said. "I went to school with both Lee and Martha Kendrick…his sister."

"Where is he?"

Wales had stared. "Back on Earth, at Westpenn Observatory. He said he'd be along soon."

The Secretary said, "He's not at the Observatory. He hasn't come to Mars yet, either. He's disappeared."

"But, why…"

"I don't care *why*, Wales. I want to know *where*. Kendrick's got to be found. His disappearance is affecting the Evacuation. That's the report I get from a dozen different men back on Earth. I message them, 'Why are the

6

rocket-schedules falling behind?' I tell them, 'it's Doomsday Minus 122, and Evacuation must go faster.' I get the answer back, 'Kendrick's disappearance responsible...are making every effort to find him.'"

After a silence the Secretary had added, "You go back to Earth, Wales. You find Kendrick. You find out what's slowing down Evacuation. We've *got* to speed up, man! There's over twelve million people still left on Earth."

And here he was, Wales thought, in a rocket-ship speeding back to Earth on one of the endless runs of the Marslift, and he still didn't know why Evacuation had slowed, or what Lee Kendrick's disappearance had to do with it, and he'd have precious little time to find out.

THEY WERE SWEEPING in in a landing-pattern now, and the turquoise had become a big blue balloon fleeced with white clouds. And Hollenberg was far too busy with his landing to talk now. The rocket-captain seemed, indeed, relieved not to be questioned.

The rush inward, the roar of air outside the hull, the brake-blasts banging like the triphammers of giants, the shadowed night side of the old planet swinging up to meet them...

When he stepped out onto the spaceport tarmac, Wales breathed deep of the cool night air. Earth air. There was none like it, for men. No wonder that they missed its tang, out there on Mars. No wonder old women in the crowded new cities out there still cried when they talked of Earth.

He braced back his shoulders, buttoned the tunic of his UN uniform. He wasn't here to let emotion run away with him. He had a job. He got onto one of the moving beltways and went across the great spaceport, toward the high, gleaming cluster of lights that marked the port headquarters.

Far away across the dark plain loomed the massive black bulks of rocket-ships. Dozens of them, hundreds of them. And more were coming in, on rigid landing-schedule. The sky above, again and again, broke with thunder and the great ships came riding their brake-jets of flame downward.

Wales knew, to the last figure, how many times in the last years ships had risen from this spaceport, and how many times, having each one carried thousands of people to Mars, they had returned. Tens of millions had gone out from here. And New Jersey Spaceport was only one of the many spaceports serving the Evacuation. The mind reeled at the job that had been done, the vast number who had been taken to that other world.

And it was still going on. Under colored lights, Wales saw the long queue of men, women, and children moving toward one of the towering ships nearby. Signals flashed. Loudspeakers bawled metallically.

"...to Ship 778! All assigned to Ship 778 this way! Have your evacuation-papers ready!"

Wales went by these people, not looking at their faces, not wanting to see their faces.

The noise and crowded confusion got worse as he neared the Administration Building. Near it the buses were unloading, the endless cargoes of people, people...always people, always those pale faces.

An armed guard outside Administration's entrance looked at Wales' uniform and then at his credentials, and passed him through.

"Port Coordinator's office straight ahead," he said.

The interior of the building was a confusion of uniformed men, and women, of clicking tabulating machines, of ringing phones.

Wales thought that here you felt the real pulse of the Marslift. A pulse that had quickened now...like the pulse of a dying man.

Bourreau, the Port Coordinator, was a stocky, bald sweating man, who had thrown off his uniform jacket and was drinking coffee at his desk when Wales came in.

"Sit down," he said. "Heard you were coming. Heard the Secretary was sending you to burn our tails."

"Nothing like that," said Wales. "He just wants to know, why the devil are Evacuation schedules falling behind?"

Bourreau drained his cup, set it down, and wiped his mouth. "Listen," he said, "you don't want to talk to me."

"I don't?"

"No, I'm the Port Coordinator, that's all. I've passed millions of people through here. Evacuation Authority sends them in here, from the marshalling point over in New York. Good people, not-so-good people, and people that aren't worth saving. But to me, they're all just units. They reach here, I shoot them out. That's all. The man you want to talk to is John Fairlie."

"The regional Evacuation Marshal?"

"Yes. Talk to him, over in New York. I've got a car and driver ready for you."

WALES STOOD UP. It was obvious that Bourreau had been all ready for him, and was not going to take a rap for anybody. It was equally obvious that he'd learn nothing about Kendrick's disappearance from this man.

"All right," he said. "I'll see Fairlie first."

The driver of the car, a UN private, turned off on a side road almost as soon as they left the spaceport.

"No use bucking all the buses and trucks on the evacuation thruways," he said. "We use the old roads when we want to hurry. No traffic on *them* now."

The old roads. The ribbons of concrete and asphalt that once had carried thousands of cars, day and night. Now they were dark and empty.

The car went through a village. It too was dark and empty. They swung on through countryside, without a light in it. And then there was a bigger village, and its dark windows stared at them like blind eyes.

"All evacuated," said the driver. "Every village, town, farm, between here and New York was closed out two-three years ago."

Wales, sitting hunched by the open window, watching the road unreel, saw an old farmhouse on the curve ahead. The headlights caught it, and he saw that all its window shutters were closed. Someone, some family, had left that house forever and had carefully shuttered its windows…against doomsday.

The poplars and willows and elms went by, and now and again there was a drifting fragrance of flowers, of blossoming orchids. Old apple-trees, innocently ignorant of world's end, were preparing to fruit once more.

Wales felt a sharp, poignant emotion. He asked himself, as a world had been asking for five years: *Why did it have to be?*

There was only one answer. Far out in the dark lonesomeness of the solar system, far beyond man's new Martian colonies, the thousands of asteroids that swung in incredibly intricate and eccentric orbits…they were the answer. They had been shuttles, weaving fate's web.

Kendrick had been the first to see it, to note the one big asteroid whose next passage near Jupiter would make its eccentricity of orbit *too* great. With camera and telescope Kendrick had watched, and with the great electronic calculators he had plotted that orbit years ahead, and…

Wales had often wondered what Lee Kendrick had felt like when the first knowledge came to him, when the first mathematical formulae of doom came out on the calculator printing-tape. Mene, Mene, Tekel, Upharsin, spelled out in an equation. An electronic computer, passionately prophesying the end of man's world...

"In five years, the eccentricity of the asteroid Nereus will bring it finally across Earth's orbit at a point where it will collide with Earth. This collision will make our planet uninhabitable."

He well remembered the first stupefaction with which the world had received the announcement, after Kendrick's calculations had been proved beyond all doubt.

"No force available to us can destroy or swerve an asteroid so big. But in five years, we should be able to evacuate all Earth's people to Mars."

Kendrick, Wales thought now, had been able to give Earth the years of advance warning that meant escape, the years in which the tens of thousands of great rocket-ships could be built and the Marslift get under way. If mankind survived, it would be due to Kendrick's warning. Why should he vanish now?

Wales suddenly became conscious that his driver was putting on the brakes. They were in the outskirts of Morristown.

The streets here were *not* all dark and dead. He saw the glimmer of flashlights, the movement of dark figures, and heard calling voices.

"I thought you said these cities were all closed out?" Wales said.

The driver nodded. "Yeah. But there's still people around some of them. Looters." He stopped. "We'd better detour around here."

"Looters?" Wales was astounded. "You mean, you don't stop them?"

"Listen," said the driver. "What difference does it make what they take, when the place is closed out?"

Wales had forgotten. What difference did it make, indeed? The nearly-deserted Earth was any man's property now, when inevitable catastrophe was rushing toward it.

A thought struck him. These folk couldn't expect to take loot with them when they were evacuated. So they didn't plan to *be* evacuated.

He said, "Wait here. I'm going to have a look at them."

"I wouldn't," said the driver hastily. "These people..."

"Just wait," said Wales crisply.

He walked away from the car, toward the flashlights and the shadows and the shouting voices.

The voices had a raw edge of excitement in them, and a few were thick with alcohol. They were mixed men and women, and a few yelping youngsters.

They weren't breaking windows. They simply used crowbars to force open doors. Many doors weren't even locked. Eager hands passed out a motley collection of objects: small appliances, liquor bottles, canned synthefood, clothing.

No wonder Evacuation was going off schedule, thought Wales! Letting people play the fool like this...

A flashlight beam flared beside him, a man's face peered at his uniform, and a loud voice bellowed close to his ears, "Look, everybody! It's an Evacuation Officer!"

There was a dead silence, and then the flashlights converged on him. Somewhere in the group, a woman screamed.

"They're after us! They're going to put us on the ships and take us away!"

"Kill the bastard, knock him down!" yelled a raging voice.

Wales, too astounded to defend himself, felt a sudden shower of clumsy blows that sent him to his knees.

CHAPTER TWO

IT WAS THE VERY NUMBER of Wales' attackers that saved him. There were too many of them, they were too eager to get at him. As he hit the pavement, they dropped their flashlights and crowded around in the dark, getting in each other's way, like frantic dogs chivvying a small animal.

A foot trampled his shoulder and he rolled away from it. All around him in the dark were trousered legs, stumbling over him. Voices yelled, "Where is he?" They yelled, "Bring the lights!"

The lights, if they came, would mean his death. A mob, even a small mob like this one, was a mindless animal. Wales, floundering amid the dark legs, kept his head. He shouted loudly,

"Here come the Evacuation trucks...here they come! We'd better beat it!"

He didn't think it would work, but it did. In that noisy, scuffling darkness, no one could tell who had shouted. And these people were already alarmed.

The legs around him shifted and stamped and ran away over the pavement. A woman screeched thinly in fear. He was alone in the dark.

He didn't think he would be left alone for long. He started to scramble to his feet, beside the curb, and his hand went into an opening—a long curbside storm sewer drain.

A building was what he had had in mind, but this was better. He got down on his belly and wormed sidewise into the drain. He lay quiet, in a concrete cave smelling of old mud.

Feet came pounding back along the streets, he glimpsed beams of light angling and flickering. Angry voices yelled back and forth. "He's not here. He's got away. But there must be other goddamned Evacuation men around. They're going to round us up…"

"By God, nobody's going to round me up and take me to Mars!" said a deep bass voice right beside Wales.

Somebody else said, "All that nonsense about Kendrick's World," and added an oath.

Wales lay still in his concrete hole, nursing his bruised shoulder. He heard them going away.

He waited, and then crawled out. In the dark street, he stood, muddy and bruised, conscious now that he was shaking.

What in the world had come over these people? At first, five years ago, it had been difficult to convince many that an errant asteroid would indeed ultimately crash into Earth. Kendrick's first announcement had been disbelieved by many.

But when all the triple-checking by the world's scientists had confirmed it, the big campaign of indoctrination that the UN put on had left few skeptics. Wales himself remembered how every medium of communication had been employed.

"Earth will not be destroyed," the UN speakers had repeated over and over. "But it *will* be made uninhabitable for a long time. The asteroid Nereus will, when it collides, generate such a heat and shock wave that nothing living can survive it. It will take many years for Earth's surface to quiet again after the catastrophe. Men…all men…must live on Mars for perhaps a whole generation."

People had believed. They had been thankful then that they had a way of escape from the oncoming catastrophe…that the colonization of Mars had proceeded far enough that it could serve as a sanctuary for man, and that modern manufacture of synthetic food and water from any raw rock would make possible feeding all Earth's millions out on that arid world.

They had toiled wholeheartedly at the colossal crash program of Operation Doomsday, the building of the vast fleet of rocket-ship transports, the construction and shipping out of the materials for the great new prefab Martian cities. They had, by the tens and hundreds of millions, gone in their scheduled order to the spaceports and the silver ships that took them away.

But now, with millions still left on Earth, there was a change. Now skepticism and rebellion against Evacuation were breeding here on Earth.

It didn't, Wales thought, make sense!

He was suddenly very anxious to reach New York, to see Fairlie.

HE WENT BACK along the dark street to the main boulevard, where the little white route signs glimmered faintly. He looked for the car, but did not see it.

Shrugging, Wales started along the highway. He couldn't be too far from the big Evacuation Thruways.

He had gone only a few blocks in the dark, when lights suddenly came on and outlined him. He whirled, startled.

"Mr. Wales," said a voice.

Wales relaxed. He walked toward the lights. It was the car, and the driver in the UN uniform, parked back in an alley.

"I thought you were back at the spaceport by now," Wales said sourly.

The driver swore. "I wasn't going to run away. But no use tackling that crowd. Didn't I warn you? An Evacuation uniform sets them crazy."

Wales got in beside him. "Let's get out of here."

As they rolled, he asked, "When I left Earth four years ago, there didn't seem a soul who doubted Doomsday. Why are these people doubtful now?"

The driver told him, "They say Kendrick's World is just a scare, that it's not going to hit Earth after all."

"Who told them that?"

"Nobody knows who started the talk. Not many believed it at first. But then people began to say, 'Kendrick was the one who predicted Doomsday...if he really believed it, *he'd* leave Earth!'"

"What did Kendrick say to that?"

"He didn't say anything. He just went into hiding, they say. Leastwise, the officials admitted he hadn't gone to Mars. No wonder a lot of folks began to say, 'He *knows* his prediction was wrong, that's why he's not leaving Earth!'"

Wales asked, after a time, "What do you think, yourself?"

The driver said, *"I'm* going out on Evacuation, for sure. So maybe Kendrick and the rest are wrong? What have I got to lose? And if the big crash does come, I won't be here."

Dawn grayed the sky ahead as the car rolled on through more and more silent towns. It took to a skyway and as they sped above the roofs, the old towers of New York rose misty and spectral against the brightening day.

In the downtown city itself, they were suddenly among people again. They were everywhere on the sidewalks and they were a variegated throng. Workers and their families from the Midwest, lumbermen and miners from the north, overweight businessmen, women, children, babies, dogs, birds in cages, a shuffling, slow-moving mass of humanity walking aimlessly up and down the streets, waiting their call-up to the buses and the spaceports and the leaving of their world.

Evacuation Police in their gray uniforms were plentiful, and to Wales' surprise they were armed. Only official cars were in the streets, and Wales noticed the frequent unfriendly looks his own Car got from faces here and there in the throngs. He didn't suppose people would be too happy about leaving Earth.

The big new UN Building, towering over the city, had been built thirty years before to replace the old one. He had supposed it would be an empty shell, now that the whole Secretariat was out on Mars. But it wasn't. Here was Evacuation headquarters for a whole part of America, and the building was jammed with officials, files, clerks.

He was expected, it seemed. He went right through to the regional Evacuation Marshal's office.

JOHN FAIRLIE was a solid, blond man of thirty-five or so, with the kind of radiant strength, health, and intelligence that always made Wales feel even more lanky and shy than he really was.

"We've been discussing your mission here," Fairlie said bluntly. He indicated the three other men in the room. "My friends and fellow-officials…they're assistants to Evacuation Marshals of other regions. Bliss from Pacific Coast, Chaumez from South America, Holst from Europe…"

They were men about Fairlie's age, and Wales thought that they were anxious men.

"We don't resent your coming, and you'll get 100 percent cooperation from all of us," Fairlie was saying. "We just hope to God you can get Evacuation speeded up to schedule again. We're worried."

"Things are that bad?" said Wales.

Bliss said gloomily, "Bad…and getting worse. If it keeps up, there's going to be millions still left on Earth when Doomsday comes."

"What," asked Wales, "do you think ought to be done first?"

"Find Kendrick," said Fairlie promptly.

"You think his disappearance that important?"

"I *know* it is." Fairlie strode up and down the office, his physical energy too restless to be still. "Listen, Wales. It's the fact that Kendrick, who first predicted the catastrophe, hasn't himself left Earth that's deepening all these doubts. If we could find Kendrick and show people how he's going to Mars, it would discredit all this talk that his prediction was a mistake, and that he knows it."

"You've already tried to find him?"

Fairlie nodded. "I've had the world combed for him. I wish I could guess what happened to him. If we could only find his sister, even, it might lead to him."

Yes, Wales thought. Martha and Lee Kendrick had always been close. And now they had vanished together.

He told Fairlie what had happened to him in the Jersey City. Neither Fairlie nor the others seemed much surprised.

"Yes. Things are bad in some of the evacuated regions. You see, once we get all the listed inhabitants out, we can't go back to those places. We haven't the time to keep going over them. So others...the ones who don't want to go...can move into the empty towns and take over."

"*Why* don't they want to go?" Wales studied the other's face as he asked the question. "Five years ago, everyone believed in the crash, in the coming of Doomsday. Now people here are skeptical. You say that Kendrick might convince them. But what made them skeptical, in the first place?"

Fairlie said, "I don't know, not for sure. But I can tell you what I think."

"Go ahead."

"I think it's secret propaganda at work. I think Evacuation is being secretly sabotaged by talk that Doomsday is all a hoax."

Wales was utterly shocked. "Good God, man, who would do a thing like that? Who would want millions of people to stay on Earth and die on Doomsday?"

Fairlie looked at him. "It's a horrible thought, isn't it? But fanatics will sometimes do horrible things."

"Fanatics? You mean…"

Fairlie said, "We've been hearing rumors of a secret organization called The Brotherhood of Atonement. A group…we don't know how large, probably small in numbers…who seem to have been crazed by the coming of Doomsday. They believe that Nereus is a just vengeance coming on a sinful Earth, and that Earth's sins must be atoned by the deaths of many."

"They're preaching that doctrine openly?" Wales said, incredulous.

"Not at all. Rumors is all we've heard. But…you wondered who would want millions of people to stay on Earth till Doomsday. That's a possible answer."

It made, to Wales, a nightmare thought. Mad minds, unhinged by the approach of world's end, cunningly spreading doubt of the oncoming catastrophe, so that millions would doubt, and would stay…and would atone.

BLISS SAID, "The damn fools, to believe such stuff! Well, if they get caught on Earth, it'll be the craziest, most ignorant and backward part of the population that we'll lose."

Fairlie said wearily, "Our job is not to lose anybody, to get them all off no matter who or what they are."

Then he said to Wales, with a faint smile, "Sorry if we seem to be griping too much. I expect your job on Mars hasn't been easy either. Things are pretty tough there, aren't they?"

"They're bound to be tough," said Wales. "All those hundreds of millions, and more still coming in. But we'll make out. We've got to."

"Anyway, that's not my worry," Fairlie said. "My headache is to get these stubborn, ignorant fools who don't want to go, off the Earth."

Wales thought swiftly. He said, after a time, "You're right, Kendrick is the key. I came here to find him and I've got to do it."

Fairlie said, "I hope to God you can. But I'm not optimistic. We looked everywhere. He's not at Westpenn Observatory."

"Lee and Martha and I grew up together in that western Pennsylvania town," Wales said. "Castletown."

"I know, we combed the whole place. Nothing."

"Nevertheless, I'll start there," said Wales.

Fairlie told him, "That's all evacuated territory, you know. Closed out and empty, officially. Which means…dangerous."

Wales looked at him. "In that case, I'll want something else to wear than this uniform. Also I'll want a car…and weapons."

It was late afternoon by the time Wales got the car clear of the metropolitan area, out of the congested evacuation traffic. And it was soft spring dusk by the time he crossed the Delaware at Stroudsburg and climbed westward through the Poconos.

The roads, the towns, were empty. Here and there in villages he saw gutted stores, smashed doors and windows…but no people.

As the darkness came, from behind him still echoed the boom of thunder, over and again repeated, of the endless ships of the Marslift riding their columns of flame up into the sky.

By the last afterglow, well beyond Stroudsburg, he looked back and thought he saw another car top a ridge and sink swiftly down into the shadow behind him.

Wales felt a queer thrill. Was he being followed? If so, by whom? By casual looters, or by some who meant to thwart his mission? By the society of the Atonement?

He drove on, looking back frequently, and once again he thought he glimpsed a black moving bulk, without lights, far back on the highway.

He saw only one man that night, on a bridge at Berwick. The man leaned on the rail, and there was a bottle in his hand, and he was very drunk.

He turned a wild white face to Wales' headlights, and shook the bottle, and shouted hoarsely. Only the words, "...Kendrick's World..." were distinguishable.

Sick at heart, Wales went by him and drove on.

CHAPTER THREE

ALL THAT NIGHT, his car rolled across an unlighted, empty world. Wary of the great thruways, he followed the lesser roads. And every village, every town, every hillside or valley farm, was dark and silent. All this area that included Pennsylvania had been evacuated two years ago, and the people of these houses were now living the new life in the sprawling new cities on another planet.

Twice Wales stopped his car and cut the motor and lights, and waited, listening. Once he was sure that he heard a distant humming from far back along the highway, but it fell silent, and though he waited with gun in hand, no one came. So each time he drove on, but he could not rid himself of the conviction that someone followed him secretly.

With morning, his spirits lifted a little. He was only an hour's drive from the old Pennsylvania-Ohio line where the town of Castletown was. And there, if anywhere, he must find the trail to Lee and Martha Kendrick.

Kendrick, to the world, had become identified with the asteroid that was plunging ever nearer in its fateful orbit. It had, from the first, been called Kendrick's World. Kendrick, if anyone could, might convince those who had begun to doubt Doomsday. If Kendrick could be found...

Wales drove down a winding hillside road into the town of Butler, ten minutes later...and ran smack into a barricade.

The moment he saw the cars drawn up to block the highway, he tried to swing around fast. But he wasn't quick enough.

A voice said, "Kill the motor and get out."

Men had come out of the bushes that, in two years, had grown up close to the highway. They were unshaven men, wearing dirty jeans, with rifles in their hands. There were two on one side of the highway, and an older man on the other.

Wales looked at their dusty faces. Then he cut the motor and got out of the car.

They took his weapons, and the older man said. "You can put your hands down now. And come along with us."

"Where?"

"You'll see."

One man remained, searching Wales' car. The other two, their rifles on the ready, walked beside Wales down the long winding hill highway into the old town.

"I thought all these towns were evacuated," said Wales.

"They were, a long time ago," said the older man.

"But you men—"

"We're not from here. Now anything more you want to know, you ask Sam Lanterman. He'll have some things to ask *you*."

The main street of the town looked to Wales vaguely like a gypsy camp. Dusty cars were parked double along it, and there was a surprising number of men and women and kids about. The men all carried rifles or wore belted pistols. The children were pawing around in already-looted stores and most of the women looked with a blank, tired stare at Wales and his guard.

They took him into the stone courthouse. In the courtroom, dimly lighted and smelling of dust and old oak, four men were seated around what had once been a press-table. One of Wales' captors spoke to the man at the head of the table.

"Got a prisoner, Sam," he said importantly. "This fellow. He was driving from the east."

"From the east, was he?" said Lanterman. "Well, now, he might just have come from the south and swung around town, mightn't he?"

He looked keenly at Wales. He was a gangling man of forty with a red face and slightly bulging blue eyes that had a certain fierceness in them. The others at the table were two heavy men who looked like farmers, and a small dark vicious-looking young man.

"You didn't," said Lanterman, "just happen to come from Pittsburgh, did you?" They all seemed to watch him with a certain tenseness, at this.

Wales shook his head. "I came from the east, all the way across state."

"And where were you heading?"

WALES DIDN'T LIKE the implications of that "were". He said, "To Castletown. I'm looking for my girl. It's where she used to live."

"People in Castletown been gone two years." Lanterman said promptly. "To Mars—the damn fools!" And he suddenly laughed uproariously.

More and more worried, Wales said, "She wrote me she wasn't going to leave till I came."

"You're not one of those Evacuation Officials, are you?" Lanterman asked shrewdly.

"A lot more likely he comes from Pittsburgh," said the dark young man.

Wales, sensing an increasing suspicion and danger, thought his safest bet was honest indignation. He said loudly,

"Look, I don't know what right you have to stop me when I'm trying to reach my girl! I'm not an Evac official and I don't know what all this talk about Pittsburgh means. Who made you the law around here?"

"Son," said Lanterman softly, "there isn't any law any more. The law left here when all the people left...all except a few who wouldn't be stampeded off Earth by a lot of moonshiny science nonsense."

Wales said, as though himself dubious, "Then you don't think there's really going to be Doomsday, like they say?"

"Do *you* think so?"

Wales pretended perplexity. "I don't know. All the big people, the Government people and all, have told us over and over on the teevee, about how Kendrick's World will hit the Earth..."

"Kendrick's so-and-so," said one of the farmer-looking men, disgustedly.

"I thought," said Wales, "that I'd see if my girl was going to leave, before I decided."

He wondered if he weren't laying on the stupid yokel a little too thick. But he had realized his danger from the first.

All the bands of non-evacuees who remained in closed-out territory, making their own law, were dangerous. He'd found that out in Morristown only last night. And Lanterman and his men seemed especially suspicious, for some reason.

"Look," said Lanterman, and then asked, "What's your name, anyway?"

"Jay Wilson," said Wales. His name *had* been in the news, and he'd better take no chances.

"Well, look now, Wilson," said Lanterman, "you don't always want to believe what people tell you. Me, I'm from West Virginia. Had a farm there. On the TV it told us how this Kendrick had found out Earth was going to be destroyed, how everyone would have to go to Mars. My woman said, 'Sam, we'll have to go.' I said, 'Don't you get in a panic. People have always been predicting the end of the world. We'll wait a while and see.' Lot of our neighbors packed up and went off. People came to tell us we'd better get going too. I told them, I don't panic easy, I'm waiting a while."

Lanterman laughed. "Good thing I did. More'n a year went by, and the world didn't end. And then it turned out that this here Kendrick that started the whole stampede...*he* hadn't left Earth. Not him! Got all the fools flying out to Mars on his say-so, but wasn't fool enough to go himself. Fact is, people say he's hiding out so the Evacuation Officials can't make him go. Well, if Kendrick himself won't go, that predicted it all, why should we go?"

And that, Wales thought despairingly, was the very crux of the problem. Where was Lee Kendrick anyway? He must know that his remaining on Earth was being fatally misinterpreted by people like these.

Lanterman added, with a certain complacency, "All the fools went, and left their houses, cars, cities. Left 'em to those of us who wasn't fools! That's why we gathered together. Figured we might as well pick up what they'd left. We got near a hundred men together. I said. 'Boys, let's quit picking over these empty villages and take a real rich town. Let's go up to Pittsburgh.'"

One of the farmer-men said gloomily, "Only this Bauder had the idea first. *His* bunch took over Pittsburgh, as we found out."

Lanterman's eyes flashed. "But they're not going to keep it! Since we first tried it, we've got a lot more men. One or two joining us every few days. We'll show Bauder's outfit something this time!"

Of a sudden, the strangeness of the scene struck at Wales. A few years before, this quiet old country courthouse had been the center of a busy, populous town, of a county, a nation, a world.

Now world and nation were drained of most of their people. An Earth almost de-populated lay quiet, awaiting the coming of the destruction from space. Yet men who did not believe in that destruction, men in little bands, were, with the passing of all law, contending for the possession of the great evacuated cities.

Lanterman stood up. "Well, what about it, Wilson? You want to join up with us and take Pittsburgh away from Bauder? Man, the loot there'll be...liquor, cars, food, everything!"

WALES KNEW he had no real choice, that even though it was a maddening interruption to his search for Kendrick, he must pretend to accede. But he thought it best not to agree too readily.

"About Pittsburgh, I don't care," he said. "It's Castletown I want to get to...and my girl.

"Ho," said Lanterman, "I'll tell you what. You join up with us and I'll give you Castletown, all for your own. Of course, I'll still be boss of the whole region."

Wales made another attempt for information. "I've heard of this Brotherhood of Atonement," he said. "Are you with that outfit?"

Lanterman swore. "That bunch is *crazy*. No sense to 'em at all. Hell, no, we're not Atoners."

Wales said, slowly, "Well, looks like if I and my girl decide to stay, we'd better be in your bunch. Sure, I'll join."

Lanterman clapped him on the back. "You'll never regret it, Wilson. I've got some big ideas. Those that stick with me will get more'n their share of everything. Pittsburgh is only the start."

He added impressively, "You're joining at a lucky time. For tonight's when we're taking Pittsburgh."

The young, dark man snarled, "If he's a spy, then letting him know that will..."

"You're too suspicious, Harry," said Lanterman. "He's no spy. He's just a good boy, trying to get to his girl. He'll help us, and we'll help him. Fact, I'll take him along personal with me."

Wales had no illusions. He was still on probation with this bunch, and would be watched. He'd have to get away from them as soon as he could, and get on to Castletown on his search, but if he was too premature about it, he'd get a bullet.

During the rest of the day, he found himself never out of sight of Lanterman or Harry or one of the others. He ate with them, in the dusty dining-room of the town hotel. There was a waste and profusion of packaged synthefoods that bespoke the abundance of a world left for the looting.

Before dusk, all the men gathered in the main street, armed with rifles and Venn Tommy guns. The women, and the awed children, watched from the doors and windows along the street.

Lanterman, his red face gleaming in the sunset, and with two heavy pistols belted around him, spoke to the men, his voice echoing loudly along the silent street.

"We're going down and take Pittsburgh away from Bauder and then we'll have a decent place for us and our families to live," he said. "Lots of food, guns, everything—enough for years to come."

He looked down at the dark young man. "All right, Harry, you take your bunch along now. And you remember not to start things till you hear our signal."

Ten cars, with thirty-odd men in them, pulled out of the main street in the twilight. Harry was in the first car, and they headed south out of town.

Lanterman then told the others, "Rest of us better get going too, all except those that are staying to guard the women and kids. You stick along with me, Wilson."

Motors roared, all along the street. Lanterman climbed grandly into a long black limousine, and Wales followed him.

The car was full of men and gun-barrels when its driver, a leathery young chap who was chewing tobacco, pulled out along the street. The other cars, nearly a score of them, followed them. But they headed southeastward.

"We're going pretty far east," Wales protested. "Pittsburgh's south."

Lanterman chuckled. "Don't you worry, Wilson. You'll get to Pittsburgh, before the night's over."

For an hour the caravan of cars, without lights, rolled along silent roads and through dark villages.

They came to a halt in a little town that Wales couldn't recognize.

But when he saw wooden piers and the broad, glinting blackness of a river, he realized it must be one of the smaller towns a bit upriver from Pittsburgh on the Allegheny.

There were a dozen big skiffs tied to the piers, and a quartet of armed men guarding them. There were no lights, and the darkness was a confusion of shadowy men and of unfamiliar voices.

"Get your damned gun-butt out of my ribs, will you?"

WALES REALIZED that the whole party was embarking in the boats. He followed Lanterman into one of them. Lanterman said,

"Now I don't want one bit of noise from any of you. Get going."

The boats were cast off and forged out into the dark, wide river. In the moonless night, the shore was only a deeper bulk of blackness. Lanterman's boat, leading, swung across to the southern shore, and then kept close to it as they went silently downstream.

Occasional creak of oars, the voices of frogs along the bank—these were the only sounds. The deep summery, rotten smell of the river brought a powerful nostalgia to Wales.

Impossible to think that all this must soon end!

The darkness remained absolute as they went on downriver. They had entered what was once the busiest industrial region of the world, but it was desolate and black and silent now.

Wales ventured to whisper, "Why this way, instead of using the bridges?"

Lanterman snorted. "They expect us to use the bridges. Wait, and you'll see." A moment later he called. "No more rowing. Drift. And no noise!"

They drifted silently along the bank. A huge span loomed up vaguely over them. Wales thought it would be the old Chestnut Street Bridge.

He was startled when, beside him, Lanterman hooted. It was a reasonably good imitation of a screech owl, twice repeated.

A moment later, from the northern, farthest end of the big bridge, rifle-shots shattered the silence. There was a sudden confusion of firing and shouting there.

Lanterman chuckled. "Harry's right on time. He'll make enough row to bring the whole bunch there."

Presently there was a sound of motors. Cars without lights many of them, were racing along the riverside highway from downtown Pittsburgh. They rushed over the bridge, toward the distant uproar of shooting.

"That decoyed them out," Lanterman said. He gave orders, quick and fierce. "Allerman, you and Jim take your boats in here. Block the bridges, so they can't get back in a hurry."

Two skiff-loads of men darted toward the dim shore. And the rest, with Lanterman's skiff leading, moved under oars down along the riverside.

Now Wales glimpsed lights—a few dim, scattered gleams. With a shock, he saw big, black towers against the stars, and realized they were the skyscrapers of downtown Pittsburgh.

Their skiffs shot in, bumped and stopped. The men piled out, onto a cobbled levee that slanted up from the river.

Lanterman's voice rang out. "We've got 'em cold, with most of their men chasing Harry across the river! Come on! But remember…don't shoot anyone unless they show fight! Most of 'em'll join us, later."

The dark figures of the men, gun-barrels glinting in the starlight, went up the levee in a stumbling rush. Somewhere ahead, a voice yelled in alarm.

Wales, behind Lanterman, felt more than ever caught in a nightmare. These men, ignorant in their unbelief, battling for an empty city upon a world toward which doom was coming—it seemed a terrible dream from which he could not wake.

CHAPTER FOUR

THEY RAN FORWARD and were suddenly in a narrow street of tall, old business buildings. It was a gut of darkness in which the men stumbled and jostled each other, and now they heard an alarm-siren ahead.

Wales had no desire at all to become embroiled in this senseless struggle for an empty city. But with Lanterman just ahead, and men all around, he dared not try to slip away. Some of them were surely watching him.

They debouched into a broader street. A few blocks away along this wider avenue, a searchlight suddenly went into action, lighting up shop windows and building-fronts for a quarter-mile, and half-dazzling the dark, running figures of Lanterman's men. Instantly shots burst forth from beyond the searchlight. Bullets whined and whanged off stone-work, and there was the silvery crash of shattered plate-glass.

"Get back in here!" Lanterman yelled, and his men sucked back into the dark shelter of the narrower way.

One of them was holding his shoulder, and sobbing, "Damn them, they hit me—"

Wales, pressing close against a stone facade, looked out into the eerie brilliance ahead and recognized it as Liberty Avenue. He saw, across it, a shop window in which impeccably dressed dummies looked out as though in wide-eyed amazement at what was going on.

Lanterman paid no attention to the wounded man. "They're up in that big hotel near the Post Office," he said quickly. "Can't be many men left here—but we got to get to them fast, before the others hear and start back."

He told one of the farmer-men,

32

"You, Milton—take a dozen men and get around to the back of that hotel. Rest of us will take it from the front."

Wales thought that however ignorant he might be in some ways, Lanterman was a born leader. No wonder that people who had been bewildered and lost in doubts followed the red-faced man.

Two men with Venn guns hurried into a building at the corner of Liberty. A minute later, from a third-floor window, they suddenly let go. The searchlight went out.

"Come on!" yelled Lanterman. They poured out into the wide avenue and raced along it, keeping on the sidewalks on either side.

There was, suddenly, a burst of firing from ahead, that sounded muffled and distant. Then silence. They were nearly to the big hotel.

"Hold it, Sam!" came Milton's yell from the dark building. "It's all done."

Flashlights began to come on, like fireflies waking. There was a sound of women screeching from inside the hotel. Men came out of it, their hands high.

One was a burly, shock-haired man who cursed Lanterman when he saw him. "Shot two of my men, you—"

"Now quiet down, Bauder," said Lanterman. In the angling flashlight illumination, his face was sweating and exultant. "No call for any more fighting here. Wouldn't have been any, if you hadn't been so big-feelinged when we first came. Pittsburgh's big enough for all of us—long as you know I'm boss."

He turned to his men. "Half of you get back over to those bridges...tell 'em we've got Bauder and we've got Pittsburgh. They'll give up. Take them, Milton."

Whooping with triumph, the men started after Milton, into one of the dark side streets leading toward the river.

Wales started along with them. He half expected Lanterman to call him back, but the leader was too occupied with his moment of victory to remember the suspicions of hours before.

It was, Wales knew, the best chance he'd be likely to get to escape from this band. He let himself drop behind the rest of Milton's men as they ran down Ninth Street. Then, passing the mouth of an alley, he dodged into it and ran alone in darkness, cutting south to Sixth.

Wales stretched his legs toward the levee. The bridges were impassable to him, and the skiffs were his only chance. He made sure of oars in one of them, then pushed it out onto the dark river.

From northward, from the bridges, came the sound of firing. But as Wales rowed, the shots straggled into silence.

He guessed that the fighting was over and that Sam Lanterman was master of Pittsburgh.

When Wales finally stood on the dark northern shore and looked back, he saw a scattered twinkling of little lights moving amid the towering black structures that once had been a city.

He suddenly found that he was shaking, from reaction and despair. "Can anyone—*anything*—save people like that?"

To Wales, it suddenly all seemed hopeless—the mission on which he'd come back to Earth. Hopeless, to think that the ignorant, the short-sighted, the fearful, could ever be induced to leave Earth in time.

HE LOOKED UP at the star-decked sky. Out there in the void, the massive asteroid that spelled world's end was swinging ever forward on the orbit that in four months would end in planetary collision. You couldn't see it, though. And that was the trouble. People like these, influenced by someone's secret propaganda, wouldn't believe it until

Kendrick's World loomed dreadful in the heavens. And then it would be too late...

Wales turned and started up the street from the river. He'd been given a mission and he had to carry it out. Not only for the sake of all those ignorant ones who might be trapped on a doomed world, but also for the sake of his friends. Something had happened to Lee and Martha Kendrick, and he had to find them.

He went through the Northside district until, beyond the old Planetarium, he found a big garage. There were plenty of cars in it. In ten minutes, Wales was driving north.

He kept his lights off, and his speed down. He looked back often. No one followed him now.

"Whoever was trailing me," he thought, "will be a while discovering that I'm not still with Lanterman."

Again, he wondered who the secret trailers were. They hadn't tried to overtake him. They had just followed him. Was it someone who *also* wanted to find Kendrick? And for what reason?

He thought of The Brotherhood of Atonement that was still only a name to him, and felt a chill.

It was fifty miles to Castletown, and he dared not drive too fast without lights lest he run suddenly upon a block in the road. But after a while the moon rose and Wales was able to push the car a little faster.

The countryside dreamed in the moonlight. It was only in towns that the awful emptiness of the world crushed you down. Out here between fields and hills, things were as they had always been, and it did indeed seem mad folly for men to quit their planet. It was small wonder that some of them refused to do so.

Everything you saw, Wales thought, wrung your heart with a feeling of futility. That little white house with the picket fence that he swept past so swiftly—someone had labored hard to build that fence, to plant the flowers, to coddle a green lawn into being. And it had all been for nothing, the little houses, the mighty cities, all the care and toil and planning for centuries for nothing...

He would not let himself get into that frame of mind. It had not been for nothing. Out of it all, man had won for himself the knowledge that was now saving him. The cities that now seemed so futile had built the rocket fleets that for years had been taking the millions out to Mars. They had built the atomic power-plants, the great electronic food-and-water synthesizers, that would make life on Mars possible for all Earth's folk. No, man's past was not a failure, but a success.

Of a sudden, Wales' brooding was shattered as he drove into the town of Brighton Falls.

There was no town.

He pulled up, startled. In the moonlight, a blackened devastation stretched around him, a few ruined walls still standing, the rest a shapeless mass of blackened debris.

Wales, after a moment, got over his first shock. "Lightning could easily start a fire," he thought. "And with nobody to put it out..."

It seemed logical enough. Yet he still felt shocked as he drove hastily on out of the blackened ruins.

As the moon rose, he drove faster. Castletown was very near. He would soon know if he had come all this way for nothing.

In this old town, Wales had grown up with Lee and Martha Kendrick. In Westpenn College here, they'd been classmates. Lee, making astronomy his career, had stayed here at the small but famous Westpenn Observatory, to make finally the astronomical discovery of approaching Doomsday. And, Wales knew, Martha had stayed with him, keeping the old Kendrick house for him.

He knew too, that the Kendricks had stayed on here, even after the whole region was evacuated.   And then they'd disappeared.

Fairlie had said that his men had searched here and hadn't found them. But Wales clung to the conviction that his quest of them must begin here.

CASTLETOWN
A Good Place to Live

THE SIGN at the edge of town, unintentionally ironic now, went past him. It had been a long way from here, Wales thought, to the Rocket Service school out west, a long way farther to Mars, and yet here he was, after all these years, back again.

His own boyhood home was here but there was no reason at all to visit it. He was glad there was no reason, he was glad now that his parents had died before Doomsday came.

He turned off the highway. The campus of Westpenn College was on the hills east of Castletown. The buildings were dark and silent. On the loftiest eminence, the dome of the Observatory shouldered the stars. There was no light there, either.

Wales drove past the campus to the big, square, old-fashioned Kendrick house. It was dark and quiet as everything else. He stopped his car, made sure of the pistol in his jacket pocket, and ascended the steps.

He felt, after all these years, like a ghost coming back to a dead town, to a dead world. Impatient of fancies, he pushed at the front door and it swung quietly inward.

Wales flashed his light around the hall inside. Then he began going through the rooms.

Over an hour later he was back in the front hall, disappointed and baffled. He had found no one in the house, and no evidence that either Lee or Martha had been here recently.

As he stood, anxious and frustrated, Wales suddenly noticed a smear of red on the inner side of the White-painted front door.

He flashed his light on it. Two words were written in lipstick on the door, in a feminine hand. "The Castle." Nothing more.

Wales' thoughts leaped. He pulled open the door and went out to his car fast. In a moment he was driving on downtown, his hopes suddenly high.

"The Castle." That was what, when they were all kids, they had called the old hilltop mansion of an ancient great-aunt of the Kendricks'. They had given it that name because of its moor-ish wooden tower with a crenellated top, that had fascinated them.

Of a sudden, checking his elation, there came to Wales the sure knowledge that Martha had been *afraid*, when she wrote that direction.

Afraid to leave a more definite clue, than that one that only a few people could possibly understand.

"But she didn't leave that for me..." Wales thought, puzzledly. "As far as they knew, I was still on Mars. But then, for whom?"

He began to worry more deeply than before. He had found a clue to the Kendricks, a clue that Fairlie's agents had been unable to, understand, but the careful obscurity of it made their disappearance suddenly more sinister.

Wales drove fast through the familiar old hometown streets. He noticed, as he swung around the Diamond, that one store had a brave sign chalked on its window, "Closed for Doomsday".

He swung right, up North Jefferson Street, then on up the steep hill that was the highest point of Castletown. He was wire-tense with hope when he parked in front of the old wooden monstrosity of a mansion.

Everything was dark here, too. His hopes fell a little as he went up the tree-lined walk. Still, people would be careful about showing light...

Something exploded in the back of Wales' head, and his face hit the ground hard.

CHAPTER FIVE

WALES REGAINED a foggy consciousness, to become aware that someone close to him was sobbing.

He felt that he had to get up. There was something he must do. He had very little time, the end of Earth was rushing upon him, and there was someone he must find. He *must* move, get up…

"Jay," said a voice somewhere. "It's me. *Me! * Martha."

Wales got his eyes open, and saw a dark figure bending over him, and he threshed his arms numbly, trying to push it away, trying to get up, to fight.

"Jay!"

A flashlight beam suddenly sprang into being right above him, almost dazzling him. Then, his vision clearing, he saw that the beam was not on his face but on the face that bent above him.

A girl's face, quite familiar, framed by dark hair, but with tears running down it. Martha Kendrick's face.

The beam went out and the darkness was upon them again.

Wales found he was lying on damp grass, one hand resting on a concrete walk. He saw trees and a big house with a crenellated wooden tower, against the stars.

"Martha," he muttered. "So you were here. But there's someone else—someone slugged me—"

Her voice came uncertainly. "That was me, Jay. I—I might have killed you—"

He didn't understand at all. But, as his brain began to clear a little, he became aware of a pounding headache.

He sat up. Martha had her arm around his shoulders, but she seemed more to cling to him than to support him. She was sobbing again.

"How could I *know?*" she was saying. "I didn't even know you were on Earth. When your car came, when you came up the walk in the dark, I knew it wasn't Lee. Not tall enough. I thought it was one of them. I didn't dare shoot, so I used the gun to hit you—"

He gripped her arm. "Martha, where is Lee?"

"Jay, I don't know. I've been waiting for him here, hoping he'd come. I've been nearly crazy, by myself. And afraid..."

Wales perceived that she was near hysteria. And her fear communicated to him.

He got unsteadily to his feet. "We'd better go inside. Where we can talk, and have a light, without anyone seeing it."

His head felt big as a pumpkin, but he navigated the steps of the old mansion successfully. In the dark interior of the house, he heard Martha lock and chain the door. Then her hand gripped his wrist.

"This way. I have one room blacked out—the kitchen."

He let her lead him through the darkness, heard her close another door. Then her flashlight came on again, illuminating the barny old kitchen.

He looked at her. He had remembered Martha Kendrick as a small, dark girl, something of a spitfire. There was no chip on her shoulder now. She looked near collapse, her face dead white, her hands trembling.

She insisted on putting cold wet cloths on his head. Holding them there, feeling at the same time painful and a little ridiculous in appearance, Wales made her sit down with him at the kitchen table. The flashlight, lying on the table, threw angular shadows against the walls.

"How long have you been hiding here, Martha?"

"Five weeks. It seems like five years." Her lips began to quiver. "It's been like a terrible dream. This old house, the town, everything you knew all your life, deserted and strange. The little sounds you hear at night, the glow in the sky from the burnings…"

"But *why* have you hidden here? Why didn't you—and Lee too—report to New York for evacuation to Mars, like everyone else?"

Martha Kendrick seemed to get a little control of herself. She spoke earnestly.

"When Castletown, like the rest of this whole region, was evacuated two years ago, Lee wanted to stay on a while. He was working each night over at the Observatory, keeping a constant watch on Nereus. I think he kept hoping that he'd discover some change in its orbit, some hope. But—he found nothing. He'd been right. It would hit Earth."

"But why did *you* stay, too?" Wales demanded. Martha looked at him in surprise.

"Somebody had to take care of Lee. I wasn't going to Mars until he went. It was lonesome, after everybody left Castletown. Lee said we'd soon go, ourselves. But then…he changed. He began to seem terribly worried about something, terribly afraid."

"We've all been afraid," Wales said somberly, but she shook her head.

"It wasn't the crash, it wasn't Doomsday, Lee was afraid of. It was something else. He said he feared all Earth's people weren't going to get away. He said there were men who didn't *want* everyone to get away, men who wanted to see a lot of people trapped here when Doomsday comes!"

WALES WAS ELECTRIFIED out of his headachy grogginess by her statement. He grasped her wrist. "Martha, Lee said that? Who did he say they were…those who wanted to trap millions into staying here?"

Again she shook her head. "He didn't say who they were. He said he wasn't sure, it was only a suspicion. But it worried him. He went to New York once to see John Fairlie about…the regional Evacuation Marshal."

Wales thought hard. "Yes. Fairlie told me he suspected some deliberate, secret effort going on to induce millions of people to stay on Earth till it was too late. Either Fairlie got that idea from Lee, or Lee got it from him—" He broke off, then asked, "Did Lee ever talk about The Brotherhood of Atonement?"

Martha nodded. "Oh, yes, quite often. We've been afraid of them, ever since everyone else left Castletown."

Again, Wales was astonished. "What do you know about that Brotherhood, Martha?"

She seemed surprised by his excitement. "Why, Jay, they're fanatics, a superstitious movement that started long before evacuation was carried out here. People whose minds became unhinged by the coming of Doomsday. They preached down in the Diamond, I heard them; terrible ravings that Doomsday was sent us for our sins—that only sacrifice and atonement of lives and treasures would save the world. Then, when evacuation went on, here, all the Brotherhood hid in the country so they wouldn't have to go."

"And they're here now?" he exclaimed.

Martha shuddered. "Not *here*. It's the one thing I've feared most these last weeks, that they'd burn Castletown."

"Burn Castletown? Good God…why?"

Martha looked at him. "Jay, they're burning the empty cities, one by one. A sacrifice. An atonement. I'm afraid Sharon was burned two nights ago—the glow in the sky seemed to come from there. And I've seen other fire-glows in the south…"

Wales, with a sudden cold feeling, remembered the blackened desolation of Brighton Falls. Then it had been no accident? Then it had been deliberate, a purposeful thing, a sacrifice…

He suddenly saw Earth as it was. A nearly-empty planet reeling toward crazy anarchy. In New York, where there was still law and order and you could see the rocket-fleets of the Marslift coming and going methodically in the sky, it had still seemed like a civilized world. But out here in the black, blind evacuated regions was deepening chaos, with law gone and all the most atavistic passions of humanity let loose. With the ignorant and mad who refused to leave battling for the possession of deserted cities, or setting the torch to unpeopled towns in superstitious sacrifice…

He asked Martha, "Did Lee think that The Brotherhood of Atonement was behind the plot to trap people into staying on Earth?"

That seemed to startle her. "He didn't say so. But could they be the ones? Mad people like that…?"

"It would take a fanatic to perpetrate a horror like getting people trapped in Doomsday," Wales said. "But let it pass, for the moment. I want to know what *happened* to Lee."

Her dark eyes filled with tears again. "I can't tell you. It was like this. Each night, Lee went to the Observatory. I stayed in our home but I had a portable radiophone and he had one, always open, so I could call him if I needed him. But, one night five weeks ago, he called *me*. He was shouting, hoarse. He said, 'Martha, men breaking in…I think they know I suspect their plan…you get out of the house, quick! If I get away, I'll find you…'"

Her face was white and haunted, as she went on. "Jay, I didn't know what to do! I had to hide but I had to leave some word for Lee so, if he got back, he'd know where to find me. That's why I wrote "The Castle" on the door.

Nobody but he would know I meant this old house. I ran out and was only a few blocks away when I heard cars, at our house, and men calling. I kept in the back streets, in the dark, and got here. I—I've been waiting here since then. Weeks. Eternities. And—Lee hasn't come. Do you think they killed him?"

Wales gave her an honest answer. "Martha, I don't know. We'll hope they didn't. We'll try to find him. And the first question is: Who took him? Who are 'they'?"

She spoke more slowly. "I've had time to think. Lots of it. When Lee said, 'I think they know I suspect their plan...' Was he referring to his suspicion that there was a terrible plot to keep many people trapped on Earth till Doomsday? Did they realize Lee suspected them, and seize him?"

Wales' fist clenched slowly. "It's the only possible answer. Lee somehow suspected who was behind the secret propaganda that's been swaying people to remain on Earth. They grabbed him, to prevent him from telling."

He added, suddenly, "And it would serve their purpose another way! It would enable them to point out that Lee Kendrick hadn't left Earth—so that Kendrick's World must be a hoax!"

An expression of pain crossed Martha's white face. "Jay, don't call it that."

"What?"

"Kendrick's World. It's not fair. Lee discovered its new orbit, he gave the whole Earth a lifesaving warning. It's not fair to give his name to the thing that's bringing Doomsday."

HE REACHED OUT and clasped her hand. "Sorry, Martha. You're right. But we still have that question to answer. Who are 'they'...the 'they' who took Lee? Are they The Brotherhood of Atonement? Or somebody else? Who else would have any motive?"

45

His head suddenly swayed drunkenly, and he brushed his hand across his eyes. Martha uttered a little cry of distress.

"Jay, you're still not over it...the blow I gave you. Here, let me make fresh compresses."

He held her back. "No, Martha, it's not that. I'm just out, dead tired. Since I reached Earth on this mission, I've had it—and only a few hours' sleep in my car, last night."

She took his wrist. "Then you're going to sleep right now. I'll keep watch. This way...I have to put the light out when we leave the kitchen..."

Wales, following her through the dark house, felt that he was three parts asleep by the time he reached the bedroom to which she led him. His head still ached, and the headache and the exhaustion came up over him like a drowning wave.

When he woke, afternoon sunlight was slanting into the dusty bedroom. He turned, and discovered that Martha sat in a chair beside the bed, her hands folded, looking at him.

She said, "I wasn't sleepy. And it's been so long since I've had anyone..."

She stopped, faintly embarrassed. Wales sat up, and reached and kissed her. She clung to him, for a moment.

Then she drew back. "Just propinquity," she said. "You would never even look at me, in the old days."

Wales grinned. "But now you're the last girl in town."

Martha's face changed and she suddenly said, with a little rush of words, "Oh, Jay, do you sometimes get the feeling that it just *can't* happen, no matter what Lee and all the other scientists say, no matter what their instruments say, that everything we've known all our lives just can't end in flame and shock from the sky ?"

He nodded soberly. "I've had that feeling. We've all had it, had to fight against it. It's that feeling, in the ignorant, that'll keep them here on Earth until it's too late—unless we convince them in time."

"What'll it really be like for us, on Mars?" she asked him. "I don't mean all the cheery government talks about the splendid new life we'll all have there. I mean, *really.*"

"Hard," he said. "It's going to be a hard life, for us all. The mineral resources there are limitless. Out of them, with our new sciences of synthesis, we can make air, water, food. But only certain areas are really habitable. Our new cities out there are already badly crowded…and more millions still pouring in."

He still held her hand, as he said, "But we'll make out. And Earth won't be completely destroyed, remember. Someday years from now…we'll be coming back."

"But it won't be the same, it'll never be the same," she whispered.

He had no answer for that.

Packaged food made them a meal, in the kitchen. It was nearly sunset, by the time they finished.

Martha asked him then, with desperate eagerness, "We're going to try to find Lee now?"

Wales said, "I've been thinking. We'll get nowhere by just searching blindly. Fairlie's agents did that, and found no trace of Lee at all. I think there's only one way to find him."

"What?"

"Since I left New York on this mission, I was followed," Wales told her. He described the shadowy, unseen trailers who had tracked him until he fell into the hands of Lanterman's men. "Now, my mission to find Lee could well have been known. Only reason anyone would follow me is to make sure I *didn't* find him. So those who tracked me must be some of the 'they' who took Lee. The Brotherhood of Atonement, it seems sure."

He paused, then went on. "So my shadows must know what happened to Lee, where he is. If I could catch one of them, make him talk…"

"We could find out what they've done with Lee!" Martha exclaimed. Then her excitement checked. "But you said they must have lost your trail, at Pittsburgh."

He nodded. "Sure. But what would they do, when they made sure I wasn't with Lanterman's band in Pittsburgh, that I'd slipped away? Knowing that I was headed for Castletown in the first place, they'll come *here* to look for me. And I'll be waiting for them."

A little pallor came into Martha's face. "What are you going to do, Jay?"

"I'm going to set up a little ambush for them, right down in the center of, town," he said grimly. "You'll be quite safe here, until…"

SHE INTERRUPTED passionately. "No. I'm going with you." He started to argue, and then he saw the desperation in her eyes.

"Jay, you don't know what it's been like to be so alone. I'm not letting you go without me."

He said, after a moment, "Maybe you're right. But we'd better get started. Do you have a gun?"

She produced an ancient revolver. "I found this, in the house next door. I wanted something…I was so afraid the Brotherhood would come here…"

Wales nodded. "We'll get you something better than that. Now listen, Martha. You must keep silent, you must do what I say. There's no one at all to help us, if things go wrong."

She nodded. He opened the back door and they went out of the old house, and across its ragged back yard to the alley.

Wales, his gun in his hand, led the way down the alley. Where it crossed Grant Street, he stopped, stuck his head out and peered both ways. The street of old houses was still and dead. The maples along it drowsed in the dying sunlight. A little breeze whispered, and was quiet again.

Wales and Martha darted across the street fast, into the shelter of the alley again. As they went down it, hugging the backs of buildings, heading toward the Diamond, Wales had again that fantastic feeling of unreality.

He remembered every foot of these blocks. How many times, carrying a newspaper route as a boy, he had short-cutted along this alley. And how would a boy dream that he would come back to it someday, when the familiar, town lay silent and empty before approaching world's end?

They reached the Diamond, an oval of grass with benches and a Civil War monument and with the three-story storefronts all around it, their dusty windows looking down like blind eyes. "KEEP RIGHT" said a big sign at each end of the Diamond, but nothing moved along the wide street, nothing at all.

Wales peered from a doorway, then took Martha's wrist and hurried across. Dutton's Hardware, with its windows still full of fishing-tackle displays, was on the other side. But when he tried the door, it was locked.

He could smash the plate-glass of the door but that would be to advertise his presence inside. He hurried, tense and sweating now, around to the alley in back of the store. The back door by the little loading platform was locked too, but he broke a window with his gun-butt.

The shattering of the glass sounded in the silent town like an avalanche. Wales swore under his breath, waited, listened.

There was no sound. He got the window open, and drew Martha in after him into the dim interior of the store.

"Why here?" she whispered, now.

"Anyone who comes searching Castletown for me is bound to come to the Diamond sooner or later," he told her. "It's our best place to watch."

He had another reason. He went forward through the obscurity of the store, through sheaves of axe handles and rural mail-boxes in piles, with the hardware-store smell of oil and leather and paint strong in his nostrils.

He found a gun-rack. All rifles and pistols were gone but there were still a row of shotguns, the barrels gleaming in the dimness like organ-pipes. In the worn, deep wooden drawers beneath, he found shells.

"I seem to remember you used to go after pheasant with Lee," he said.

Martha nodded, and took one of the pump-guns.

"Just don't use it, until I tell you," he said.

They went on, toward the front of the store. Then they sat down, and through the show-windows they could look out on the Diamond.

The sun sank lower. The man on the monument cast a longer and longer shadow across empty benches where once old men of Castletown had gossiped.

Nothing happened.

Wales, waiting, thought how outraged crusty Mr. Dutton would have been by what they'd done. It had been like him to carefully lock up the store, front and back, before he left it forever.

He looked across the Diamond, at the Busy Bee Cafe, at the Electric Shoe Repair Shop, at the old brick YWCA.

Twilight deepened. Martha moved a little, beside him. He hoped she wasn't losing her nerve. Then he realized she had been nudging him. She whispered, "Jay."

At the same moment he heard a thrumming sound. Even here inside the store, it seemed unnaturally loud in the silent town. He crouched lower.

A long green car came down the street and swung around the Diamond, and then with squealing brakes it came to a stop.

The hunters had come to Castletown.

CHAPTER SIX

THREE MEN GOT OUT of the car and stood there in the dusk, at the south side of the Diamond.

They wore windbreakers and slacks. One of them was short and pudgy, the other two were average-looking men. All of them carried Venn guns.

They talked, briefly. One of the average men seemed to be the leader, Wales thought, from the way he gesticulated and spoke.

"What are they going to do?" whispered Martha.

"Look for me," Wales said. "A hundred to one they've left a man at the Observatory, and at your home—in case I come there. And these three are going to search downtown for me."

The three separated. One walked east along Washington Street. The other one got back into the car and drove off on North Jefferson. The remaining man—the dark-haired pudgy one, started going around the Diamond, keeping close to the fronts of the stores, ready to dart into cover at any moment.

An idea came to Wales, and he acted upon it at once. He crept to the front door of the hardware store, unlocked it, and silently opened it a few inches.

He came back, rummaged frantically in the dimness of the shelves till he found a spool of wire. Then he told Martha,

"Come on, now…get down behind this counter. And stay there."

"Jay, he's coming this way!" she protested. "He'll see the door ajar—"

He interrupted, "Yes, I want him to. Do as I say."

Her face white in the dusk, she got down behind the counter, back in the middle of the store.

Wales crept swiftly to the front of the store, whipped behind the counter there, and crouched down.

Now, with the door ajar, he could hear the pudgy man coming along the sidewalk. Then he saw him, his heavy, doughy face turning alertly from side to side as he came along.

The man stopped and the Tommy gun in his hands came up fast. He had seen the hardware-store door was a little open.

With the gun held high, the pudgy man came slowly to the door. His foot kicked it wide open. He peered into the dimness of the store, poised on his feet like a dancer, ready to turn instantly.

Wales' fingers closed on a little carton of hinges, under the counter. He suddenly hurled the little box toward the other side of the store. It struck a display of tinware with a tremendous clatter.

The pudgy man whirled toward that direction, in a flash.

With a movement as swift, Wales darted out in the same moment and jammed his pistol into the pudgy man's back.

"Let go of that gun," Wales said, "or I'll blow your spine out!"

He saw the pudgy man stiffen and arch his back in a convulsive movement. Wales' finger tightened on the trigger. But, before he pulled it, the Tommy gun clattered to the floor.

"Martha," said Wales.

She came, fast, her face white and scared in the dusk.

"Take this wire and tie his wrists behind him," Wales said. "Don't get in front of my gun."

With shaking fingers, she did as he ordered. "Now shut the front door."

Wales turned the pudgy man around. "Now sit down, on the floor. First sound you make above a whisper, you're dead."

The pudgy man spoke, in a high falsetto whisper. "You're dead, right now. Whatever happens to me, you won't get out of Castletown."

"Don't worry about us," Wales advised. "Worry about yourself. Where's Lee Kendrick?"

The pudgy man looked at him calmly. "I don't know what you're talking about."

Martha whispered, with astounding fierceness, "Make him tell, Jay."

WALES FIRST SEARCHED their prisoner. He found no papers on him at all, nothing but clips for the gun. Pudgy seemed quite unperturbed.

"All right, where's Kendrick?" Wales said again.

Pudgy said, "You talking about the Kendrick that discovered Doomsday coming? *The* Kendrick? How should I know?"

"Who are you working for?" Wales persisted. "Who took Kendrick, who sent you to follow me here from New York. The Brotherhood?"

Pudgy looked at him in blank surprise. "Huh?"

"The Brotherhood of Atonement," Wales said. "You're one of them, aren't you? They've got Kendrick, haven't they? Where?"

Pudgy's face split in the beginnings of a guffaw. Wales raised his pistol quickly, and the man choked off the laugh. But his sides shook.

"'Me one of that Brotherhood? You're funny. You're really funny, Wales."

"So you know me," Wales snapped. "You know all about me, you came trailing me when I started to hunt for Kendrick. Who sent you?"

A queer gleam came into the eyes of Pudgy, but he remained silent.

Something in that look made Wales whirl around. Their prisoner sat facing the store-front.

Out there in the dusk, one of the two other men had come back into the Diamond.

"Martha," whispered Wales.

"Yes?"

"Take your shotgun. If he tries to open his mouth, bring it down on his head."

Promptly, she picked up the shotgun and stood with it raised. Pudgy looked up at her, and winced.

Wales crept back to the front of the store and looked out. The other man out there seemed worried, holding his Venn gun high and looking slowly all around the Diamond. That he was worried by Pudgy's absence, Wales knew.

The man out there got into cover behind the pedestal of the monument, and waited. Waiting, obviously, for the man with the car to come back.

Minutes passed. The twilight was deepening into the soft May darkness. Suddenly Martha whispered.

"Jay!"

He swung around. Her face was a queer white blur in the darkness. "What?"

"I hear singing," she said. "Someone is singing, away off."

"Just the wind in the wires," he said. "There's no one in the whole town but us...and them. You keep your eye on that fellow. I think we're due for trouble soon."

He waited again. From outside, he could hear the sound of the wind rising and falling. Then a strange conviction crept over him.

It was not the wind. It was the rise and fall of distant voices, many of them. Now the breeze brought it through the night a little louder, now it ebbed back to a murmur. Carefully, Wales opened the door a crack to listen.

He exclaimed, "It's from up on North Hill, but what in the world..."

He suddenly crouched lower again, his pistol raised. Down the hill along North Jefferson came the long green car, racing fast.

It swung around the Diamond. The man in it leaned out and called. The man behind the monument ran out to meet him, talking fast and gesticulating.

But the driver of the car pointed northward and shouted. Wales could not see his face but he could hear the raw tone of his voice, and caught the one final word, "...coming!"

The other man leaped into the car, after a last look around the empty Diamond. The car shot away down Washington, heading east.

"Why, they've gone, run away!"

Martha exclaimed. "They left their partner here and—" Wales held up his hand. "Listen!"

As the roar of the receding car died away, the sound of singing came again—and this time it was louder, much louder, and there was a steady throb of drums beneath it.

It rolled down from the north and he thought now he could hear the words of a chorus, endlessly repeated.

"Halle-lu-jah! Halle-lu-jah..."

Lights suddenly sprang into being up there on the crest of North Jefferson Street hill. They were not steady lights, they were moving, tossing and shaking, and there were dozens, scores of them. They were torches.

A long, thick snake of burning torches came down the wide street into the dark and lifeless town. Wales could see no people, only the torches, scores of them, hundreds of them. But he could hear the loud chanting of the people who carried those lighted brands.

"*Halle-lu-jah...*"

Crash-crash-boom, thundered drums from the forefront of the river of torches, and Wales felt a wild quickening of their beat and of the chanting voices, that checked his breathing.

Martha uttered a low cry. "Jay, it's the Brotherhood coming! The fanatics coming *here* now, to—" The hair bristled on Wales' neck. She did not need to finish the horrified exclamation. The nightmare shape of the looming event was only too clear.

From town to town The Brotherhood of Atonement marched, those weak, crazed minds unhinged by the coming of Doomsday. Brighton Falls they had burned, and Sharon, and God knows how many other deserted towns. And now it was the turn of Castletown to be a sacrifice and an atonement...

He wanted to turn and flee from that mad, oncoming parade. But he did not. He crouched, watching, and he felt Martha, beside him, shivering.

"Jay, if they have Lee—he might be with them!"

"That's what I'm hoping for," he whispered.

NOW THE TORCHES were coming down into the Diamond, and now he could see the people who carried them. They started around the oval, and the tossing of the red burning brands was flashed back from the windows all around, that shone like big eyes watching in amazement.

First, ahead of the torches, marched a half-dozen men and women with drums, beating a heavy, absolutely unvarying rhythm. After them came the main mass. He thought there might be two to three hundred of them.

Men, women, children. Torn and dusty clothes, unkempt hair, unshaven faces, but eyes glittering with a wild, rapt emotion, voices shouting the endless chorus of The Brotherhood of Atonement...

Halle-lu-jah!"

These crazed fanatics were gripped by no religious passion. The religious folk of the world had seen God's hand in the saving of Earth's peoples by man's newly-won knowledge. But these shouting marchers had gone back to dark barbarism, to pagan propitiation of a threatening fate, back beyond all civilization.

Boom-boom crashed the drums, right in front of the Dutton store, as the van of the mad parade swept past, following a tightening path around the oval, making room for more and more of the torch-bearers here in the center of the old town. And presently they were all in the Diamond, a packed mass of wild faces and shaken torches, all turned toward the center where the monument stood.

A man with a white face and burning eyes leaped up onto the pedestal of the monument, and the drums banged louder and a great cry went up from the Brotherhood. He began to speak, his voice shrill and high.

"Jay, do you see Lee? I can't..."

"No," Wales said. "He's not with them."

From out there, across the waving torches, came the screeching voice. "...burn the places of sin, and the powers of night and space will see the shining signs of our Atonement, and withhold their wrath..."

Martha said, "Oh, Jay, they're going to burn Castletown. Can't we stop them, somehow...?"

He took her by the shoulders. She had had too much, but he could have no hysteria now.

"Martha, we can't stop them, they'd tear us to shreds! And what *difference* does it make now? Don't you realize...in four months this town and all towns will be destroyed anyway!"

Their prisoner, back in the darkness, suddenly raised his voice. Wales leaped back, pressed his pistol against the pudgy man's body.

"You call out and you get it now!" Wales warned savagely.

Pudgy looked up at him, and said hoarsely, "Are you crazy? Those maniacs aren't friends of mine! They're going to burn this whole town like they burned others—we got to get out of here!"

The frantic fear in the man's voice was utterly sincere. And to Wales, crouching beside the captive, came a shattering enlightenment.

He said, "Then you and your pals aren't working for the Brotherhood? Then it wasn't the Brotherhood that took Lee Kendrick, after all?"

"They're maniacs!" said Pudgy, again. "For Christ's sake, Wales, are you going to let them burn us alive?"

Wales stooped, grabbed the man by the throat. "It's not the Brotherhood who took Kendrick then. All right...who was it? Who wants to see millions of people trapped on Earth? Who sent you after me? *Who?*"

Pudgy's voice turned raw and raging. "Get me out of here, and I'll tell you. But if we stay here, we're goners."

"You'll tell me right now!"

Pudgy remained sullenly silent. Then, of a sudden, the single high screeching voice out in the diamond ended, on a frenzied note.

Boom-boom, crashed out the drums again. The Brotherhood roared, as with the single voice of a mighty beast. The men with torches began to mill, to split off from the main mass, to run into the four main cross streets, shaking their firebrands and shouting.

58

One yelling woman applied her torch to the faded, canvas awning in front of the Electric Shoe Repair Parlor. The canvas blazed up, and the drums rolled again. "Jay!" cried Martha.

Wales forced Pudgy to his feet, faced him toward the front windows, and the torch-blazing chaos out beyond them.

"Martha and I are going out the back way," Wales said. "We're leaving you here tied and helpless—unless you tell!"

CHAPTER SEVEN

A THROBBING, LURID light beat in through the front windows of the store, as the flames across the Diamond swept up the fronts of old buildings. The hoarse hallelujah-chorus of the Brotherhood, the quickened booming of the drums, was louder. And the fiery light illumined the bloodless, distorted face of their prisoner as he stared up at Wales and Martha.

Wales still felt the shock of terrible surprise. He had been so sure that only the mad Brotherhood could possibly be behind the plot to seize Kendrick, the ghastly scheme to keep millions of people on Earth until Doomsday crashed down upon them. Who else but madmen would do such a thing? Who else would have any motive?

He didn't know. But their pudgy prisoner knew. And, even at the risk of trapping Martha and himself in the holocaust of Castletown, he meant to find out.

"Please," panted Pudgy. "We haven't got a chance if we stay here longer. I've seen these maniacs and their Atonements. They won't leave a building standing here!"

Wales looked at Martha's white face. "All right, Martha, we'll get going. We'll leave this fellow here." He started to turn away.

"No, it's murder!" screamed Pudgy. "You can't leave me here, my hands tied…"

"Then tell," Wales pressed. "Who seized Kendrick? Who's behind all this?"

Beads of sweat stood out on Pudgy's dough-white face. His eyes rolled horribly, and then he said hoarsely,

"Fairlie. John Fairlie. And others…"

"Fairlie? The regional Evacuation Marshal? What about him?" Wales demanded.

"He—and friends of his, other Evacuation Officials—they're the ones," Pudgy said. "They've got Lee Kendrick. They're the ones that want a lot of people left on Earth."

Furious, Wales took their prisoner by his fat throat and shook him. "All right, you had your chance," he raged. "And you tell us a brazen lie like that. By God, we *are* leaving you…"

Pudgy's voice rose almost to a scream. "It's the truth! You made me tell you, now I've done it, and you won't believe me! There's a bunch of them in it, I don't know how many. I know that besides Fairlie, there's a couple of assistant Evacuation Marshals in other countries and some minor officials and some others I don't know. I've seen them, up near New York. It's where they've got Lee Kendrick. They'd kill me for telling, and now I've told and you won't believe—"

Martha said uncertainly, "Oh, Jay, maybe he is telling the truth—maybe that's where Lee is!"

Wales exclaimed, "Don't you see what a lie it is? John Fairlie is one of the men charged with evacuating all the people off Earth…why would he and other Evacuation Officials want to trick millions into staying here?"

"Because they don't want them on Mars, because they think they're scum and ought to be left on Earth!" Pudgy cried. "I heard them talk, didn't I? Talk about how hard it's going to be for years on Mars with too many people there, already. And about how it'd be better for everyone if a lot of ignorant crumb-bums and their families weren't taken to Mars to be a load on everyone else. Didn't I hear them…"

Wales' rage at their prisoner receded, swept away by an icy tide of terrible doubt that despite himself was rising now in his mind.

HE REMEMBERED things, now. He remembered Fairlie's grim-face as he'd spoken broodingly of how hard a life it would be on Mars, with every one of Earth's millions there. He remembered the bitterly contemptuous way in which Fairlie—and Bliss and Chaumez and Holst—had spoken of the looters, the ignorant resisters, the crazy folk, whom it would be difficult to evacuate from Earth.

"Only fanatics would want to trap millions on Earth…" He, Wales, had said that. He'd been thinking then of the Brotherhood. But suppose there were other and more terrible fanatics? Fanatics who ruthlessly decided that the more backward and ignorant of Earth's millions would only be a burden in the hard years ahead, on Mars…and who secretly planned to trick those millions into staying until it was too late?

Such things had been planned and done before, by egotistical, self-appointed guardians of the public interest! And if—if this was the truth, it explained why he, Wales, had been followed, it explained why Fairlie had made him suspect the Brotherhood, it explained many things…

Halle-lu-jah! roared the chorus of howling voices, out in the streets. And the ruddy, throbbing light increased in intensity suddenly.

"Jay!" cried Martha, in tones of horror. He whirled around.

The front of the hardware store was on fire, with flames writhing around the edges of the windows, outside.

"You've got us killed!" sobbed Pudgy.

Wales, his thoughts now a chaos, realized that he dared delay no longer. He picked up the Venn gun, and then yanked their prisoner to his feet.

"Come on, Martha," he said. "Out that back window."

Pudgy stumbled awkwardly, his hands still bound behind him. They hurried back through the old store, with the fire-light beating brighter from behind them, and got through the window into the alley.

To their left flames shot skyward with a roar from the Penn Hotel, showers of sparks sailing into the darkness. A glance told Wales that the Brotherhood had fires going along whole blocks of Mercer and South Jefferson Streets.

"This way," he cried, starting down the alley that ran southward between the streets. He had Pudgy by the shoulder, but there was no need to make their terrified prisoner hurry.

Wales put everything from his mind, but the necessity of escape from the holocaust of this latest flaming Atonement. And the new suspicion in his mind was so shocking that he didn't want to think of it until he had to.

He knew the alleys and streets of Castletown, even in darkness. And they had light to guide them—more and more light throbbing up into the night sky behind them.

He cut across Mill Street, and on up southeastward to a residential street of cottages. Here, he gave Martha his pistol and had her stand guard over Pudgy while he himself looked for a car.

He found one, in the garage attached to the first cottage. He had to break through the house itself to enter the garage. The rooms were just as someone had left them, the furniture, the rugs, all the things they could not take with them in Evacuation, still in place.

Again, Wales felt a pang. Someone had toiled and planned for this little house and the things in it. And now it would not even endure until the common Doomsday—it would perish in the senseless flames.

He drove out into the street, and pushed Pudgy into the back seat. Taking no chances, he tied their prisoner's ankles too. Then, with Martha beside him, Wales drove fast up the steep streets southeast.

"Jay—look!" she cried, when they reached a crest. She was looking back. He stopped the car, and looked back with her.

The whole downtown section of Castletown blazed high toward the stars. The wind whirled sparks away in burning clouds, and a great pall of smoke lay toward them.

Southward from the center of town moved a river of torches. And from those streets, only now just kindling, above the crackle of flames came the distant boom of the Brotherhood drums, and their rising and falling chant.

Martha was crying. He put his arm around her, and turned her away from the sight.

"It doesn't mean anything, Martha. It would have only lasted the few months till Doomsday, anyway."

Yet he could understand her emotion. It had been a long time since he had lived in Castletown. But he wished his last look at the old town had not been like this.

He turned toward Pudgy. "Now you can talk. Let's have it."

Pudgy said sullenly, "I've already talked too much. You didn't believe me, anyway."

Wales' face hardened. He said, "All right. The flames will reach this residential section in an hour. We'll leave you here."

It was enough. Their prisoner's doughy face seemed to fall apart a little.

"All right!" he cried. "But what's the use telling you when you just say I'm lying?"

"Nevertheless, give it to me from the first," Wales ordered.

Pudgy said, "Look, this whole scheme to keep the crummy no-goods here on Earth...that wasn't *my* idea. Five years ago, when they were first organizing Operation Doomsday, I got a job in the Evacuation Police. I did all right. Pretty soon I was a sergeant. Then...I began to hear things about the Evacuation from one of the other sergeants."

The man paused, then went on. "Eugene—that was my friend in the Police—told me that Fairlie and some other Evacuation Officials needed some men for special secret police work. Said the work was so important and so secret nobody must know about it. I said okay, I'd like to be one of these special secret Evacuation Police. So they took me in. And Fairlie himself talked to me and a couple of others."

WALES, WATCHING Pudgy narrowly, saw him mop the sweat off his brow. "Fairlie told us, that they weren't going to be able to get *everybody* off Earth before Doomsday. He said it was impossible, there was bound to be millions would get left. He told us that he and some of the other officials in key places in the Evacuation had decided that since they were going to have to leave people, it'd be better to leave a lot of crummy hillbillies and share croppers and ignorant trash. He said they'd only make things tougher for everyone on Mars, anyway. It was better, Fairlie said, to weed them out and leave them here."

An icy feeling of terrible conviction began to grow in Wales, despite all his attempts to repel it.

He'd heard just that kind of talk, before. Not openly, but in sly whispers and hints. People who felt sure of escaping from Earth themselves had expressed aristocratic regret that *all* Earth's people must be saved, that they must be burdened on the new world by the "backward."

No one had quite dared to advocate such ideas publicly. But there were those who secretly held them. And those who did, very well might have secretly decided to see that the

65

"useless, backward" ones *didn't* escape Earth. Fairlie—and others like him—could be among them...

"Fairlie told us," Pudgy went on, "that they wouldn't prevent anyone leaving that wanted to leave. But, he said, lots of the dumber ones wouldn't want to leave if things were managed right, and that would solve the whole problem."

Martha interrupted, "But my brother...what of him? You said they had Lee?"

Pudgy nodded. "I was coming to that. Fairlie called some of us in real worried one night and told us we had to go to Castletown and grab Lee Kendrick. He said they'd been sounding Kendrick out about helping along the scheme, and that Kendrick wouldn't play ball."

"You mean," Wales said quickly, "that Fairlie and his group wanted Kendrick to *help* them trap the 'backward ones' here on Earth?"

Pudgy's head bobbed. "Near as I got it, that was it. Kendrick could make a statement kind of throwing doubt on whether Doomsday would happen...and the boobs would decide to stay. But I guess when Fairlie sounded him out a little, Kendrick was horrified at the idea, and Fairlie had to cover up fast and say he didn't mean it."

Martha clutched Wales' arm. "Jay, *that's* why Lee was so terribly worried, so anxious—that's why he wouldn't leave Earth! He was afraid such a scheme was really being planned!"

Wales could imagine that. He knew Lee Kendrick, and he knew that even a breath of suspicion of a plan so ruthless and terrible would have had a shattering effect on him.

"So," Pudgy finished, "before Kendrick could get too suspicious and start talking, we went to Castletown and grabbed him, and took him to New York. And his disappearance was nearly as good as his statement would have been—the boobs all figured Kendrick hadn't left Earth, so they would not."

"But he's alive?" Martha cried. "They haven't killed him."

Pudgy shrugged. "Not so far. Fairlie still wants him to make that statement, so all the scum will feel sure it's safe and will stay on Earth till too late."

Wales suddenly felt a revulsion from all that he had heard, from the shocking nightmare quality of it.

"It's not true, it *can't* be true!" he exclaimed. "Martha, this man had to tell some story to save his skin, and that's all he's done!"

Her face was white in the distant firelight. "Jay, people have done things like that, terrible as it is. They *have* killed millions, in the past, for just such reasons."

He knew that, too, and it was a knowledge he fought against—struggling against a cold conviction that he could not quite down.

"If Lee is still alive, Lee could tell us!" she was saying. "If we could reach him, rescue him..."

Wales turned back to the sullen-faced Pudgy. "You said that Fairlie and the others were holding Kendrick near New York. Just where?"

"Where he's right handy and near, yet where nobody can walk in on him," said Pudgy. "Bedloe's Island, in New York harbor. You know, the old Statue of Liberty Island."

Wales thought, his mind a turmoil. Now the flames were marching up the hillside streets toward them, and now the sound of drums and distant chanting came from away southward.

The Brotherhood was leaving Castletown, on their way to make some other lifeless city a fiery sign of their atonement.

"I still," said Wales, "can't believe it. But we'll prove it, one way or another. We'll go back to New York, and see if Lee is really on that island."

"You haven't got a prayer!" said Pudgy, his voice rising into a high whine. "They've got him guarded there."

"And you," Wales said, "can tell us just where the guards are and how best to pass them. Yes, you're going with us."

He ignored the man's frantic objections, and started the car. He headed eastward, to skirt the flaming city at a safe distance.

The danger ahead, the hunters who would still be seeking him, Wales ignored. What was there anywhere but danger, on an Earth rocking toward Doomsday?

CHAPTER EIGHT

THUNDER ROLLED and bellowed across the night sky, mounting to a deafening crescendo. Up into the starry heavens rose a great black bulk, climbing starward on a column of fading fire. And hardly had its echoes ebbed than the dull explosions came again, and another rocket-ship took off in the unending Marslift.

Crouching with Martha in the darkness of an old pier, with the murmuring black vagueness of the Upper Harbor in front of them, Wales looked over his shoulder at the fiery finger that pointed out to man's new home in the sky. He turned back to Martha, as she whispered to him. She was staring out over the dark water.

"I don't see any lights, Jay. Not one."

"They wouldn't show lights," he said. "They'd not advertise the fact that they're there."

"*If* they're there," she said. "If Lee's there."

He took her roughly by the shoulders. "Martha, don't lose your nerve now. Think what depends on this."

He jerked his head in the direction of the distant New Jersey Spaceport, as still another Mars-bound ship rode up in majestic thunder and flame.

"There should be twice as many ships, twice as many evacuees, going out now as there are! All the people who doubt, who hold back, who refuse to go—Lee is the key to saving them."

"But if we only had *help*, Jay! The authorities—"

Wales said, "Fairlie, as regional Evacuation Marshal, *is* the top local authority here now. And don't you see—if that story is true; Fairlie is the last man we dare let know we're here."

He took her hand. "Come on. We've still got to find a skiff of some kind."

They started along the dark waterfront. They were, Wales figured, somewhere in the southern Jersey City docks. Out in the dark harbor lay Bedloe's Island, and it was past midnight and there was little time.

He and Martha, with their prisoner, had come across Pennsylvania by unused, deserted back roads during the day. The circuitous route had taken time, and a few hours of sleep snatched in a thicket off the road had taken more time. But Wales had not dared to risk being seen.

If Pudgy's story was true, Fairlie was the enemy. Fairlie was the man who had sent hunters after him. And it would be so easy for the Evacuation Marshal, with his regional authority, to have Wales proclaimed an outlaw on some phony charge, and set every Evacuation Police post around New York looking for him.

They dared seek aid of no one. If Kendrick was a prisoner on the little island, they must attempt the rescue themselves. And that would not be easy, judging from what Pudgy had said.

Wales had driven into an alley in deserted Jersey City, and had dragged their bound prisoner into an empty store.

"Now," said Wales, "we're going to leave you here."

"Tied hand and foot?" cried Pudgy. "Why not kill me and get it over with? This town is closed out, I could yell all day and nobody would hear me. I'll starve! No one will ever come…"

"*We'll* come, and free you," Wales said. "After we've got Kendrick off that island. But of course, if we fail, if they get us, then we'll never be back. I want you to think about that."

Pudgy had thought about it, and it was clear that he did not like that thought at all. When it had sunk in, Wales said,

"Now you tell us all you know about the set-up on that island. How many guards, where they usually are, how they're armed, where Kendrick is kept. Everything. If you brief us well enough, we *may* succeed...and then we'll be back for you."

Pudgy had got the point. He had talked long and rapidly, feverishly giving Wales every scrap of information he possessed.

They had left him there, and had come by foot to the waterfront, and now if they had a boat, the island was only a little way ahead.

But there was no boat, not a canoe even, along these dark docks. Wales led the way farther along the waterfront. He dared not flash a light, and they might search all night amid these dark piers without success.

HE WAS BEGINNING to despair, when they came to a small boatyard. He found a skiff by stumbling over it in the dark. There were no oars, but he soon forced the door of the dark office shack and found those.

"Now before we start, Martha..." He was fitting the oars into locks that he'd made as silent as possible by rag mufflings. "...when we reach the island, I want you to stay on the shore and wait."

"I'm not afraid..." she began, but Wales cut her short.

"Listen, it's not that. I'll be in the dark there. If I have to shoot, I want to be sure I'm not shooting you by mistake."

He pushed out onto the water, and bent to the oars, rowing steadily. The tide was running, and he had to allow for that, but there was only a little choppiness on the Upper Harbor.

Wales thought again how unreal everything on Earth seemed by now. And this scene most of all! This harbor had once been the busiest in the world, and by night the lights of shipping, of docks, of bridges, had flared everywhere, with the electric glow of Manhattan blazing over everything.

And now there was silence and darkness on the waters. All the millions who had lived around these shores had left Earth long ago, and their cities were dark and still. Only the downtown tip of Manhattan still showed patterns of lighted windows, where the ceaseless activities of Operation Doomsday centered.

Wales rowed on, and then rested his oars a moment and turned and peered ahead in the darkness. He saw a lofty shadow now against the stars, and knew that it was the great Statue. He lifted the oars again, rowing now with infinite care to make no sound.

Brr-rumble-oom-oom-oom...

Up into the sky westward rose another of the mighty Marslift rocket-ships, and then in quick succession, two more.

The flare of them in the heavens sent a wild, shaking light over the waters, over the little skiff.

"Get down!" Wales whispered frantically, and he and Martha crouched low in the little craft.

The *oom-oom-oom* faded away in muttering echoes. Wales could but pray that they had not been seen from the island ahead, and row on.

He hoped desperately that there would be no more rocket-ships taking off, no more flares in the sky, until he reached the island. It seemed to him that he rowed eternally, and got nowhere.

Then, in the darkness, Martha whispered warning. The skiff bumped land. Wales made out a low bank rising above them. He picked up the Venn gun and climbed ashore.

He whispered, "Stay in the skiff, Martha. You can push off if I fail." And added quickly, "Don't you see, if I do fail, you'll be the last hope left."

He gave her no time to argue. He gripped the Venn gun, and started through the darkness.

There was no doubt about directions. Huge now against the stars loomed the Statue. And in it, if Pudgy had told truth, were Lee Kendrick—and the four of Fairlie's secret police who guarded him.

Wales crossed the park with his stubby gun held high. The grass was tall and ragged from long lack of care. And there was not a sound, or a light, on the little island.

He circled around to the front of the Statue, and stared up at the parapet of the mighty pedestal, and the entrance to the giant figure.

Nothing. No light, no sound of movement.

Wales felt a chill of dismay. He had not realized how much he had begun to hope, until now.

Brr-rumble...

He heard the first preliminary roar from the west, and immediately he dropped flat behind a shrub.

THE FULL THUNDEROUS diapason of take-off broke around him, and the flaming exclamation point in the heavens blazed brightly.

And Wales saw a man, with a gun under his arm, standing on the parapet.

The flare of light died, and the rocket-roar grumbled away.

But now, as he rose to his feet, Wales felt a wild triumph. The guard was there, as Pudgy had said, and that meant...

He moved forward, and started up the steps. He was more than halfway up them, moving softly, when he heard a movement above.

Wales froze. The guard above might not have heard him. But he could take no chances, with all that depended on him now.

He crouched waiting on the steps, the Venn gun raised. It seemed to him that hours, went by.

Rumble-boom-boom...

As the distant rocket-roar crashed again, as the column of fire streaked across the sky, by its light Wales saw the man on the parapet peering down toward him with his gun alertly raised.

Instantly, Wales shot him. He shot to kill.

The man dropped. Wales raced on up the steps, hoping that the brief burst of his Venn gun would not have been heard in the rocket-roar.

But a door above swung open, and light spilled out from inside the base of the giant Statue. Two men appeared in the doorway, drawing pistols.

"What—" one cried.

Wales fired a prolonged burst. He had no intention whatever of taking extra risks by sparing life. These men, and the men they worked for, would have taken the lives of millions. There was no mercy in him.

One of the two in the doorway fell. The other, blood welling from his shoulder, tried to shift his pistol to his other hand.

Wales, racing up to them, heard pounding footsteps inside the statue, and he took no time to shoot again. He clubbed the Venn gun's barrel down over the head of the wounded man, and sprang over him and the dead one in the doorway, right into the base of the lofty figure.

A light burned in here. He ran to the foot of the winding stair that led upward. Frantic feet running up above him made reverberating echoes. He glimpsed a pair of legs on the stair...

He shot, and the legs crumpled and a man came sliding back down the stair, screaming and trying to aim his gun. Wales triggered again, and when the scream of ricocheting steel and the echoes of gunfire died away, there was silence unbroken.

He started running up the stair. In a minute he heard Martha's voice calling, from down beneath.

"Jay!"

He shouted back down, and ran on, his heart pounding, his lungs pumping.

He came into the grotesque room of angled steel that was the inside of the giant head. There was a carefully shaded light here. And a man huddled on the floor near it, shackled to the wall.

WALES TURNED the light full on him. A bearded face looked at him, with wild dark eyes—a face he could hardly recognize.

"Lee?" he said. And then suddenly, he was sure. "Lee Kendrick."

Kendrick said, hesitantly, "Why it's Jay Wales. But you were on Mars. How—" And then Kendrick's eyes suddenly flamed and he shouted hoarsely. "Wales, you don't know what's happened, what they're planning..."

"I *know*," Wales said, stooping by him. "Take it easy. Please..."

Kendrick clutched him, babbling, pleading. Not until Martha came in, and stooped beside her brother, crying, could Wales get away.

He said, "Try to quiet down. There must be a key to these shackles somewhere."

He went back down the stair. The man he had shot in the shoulder and then stunned, was now stirring and groaning.

Wales made a rough bandage for the bleeding shoulder, and then tied the man's wrists with his own belt. He thought it would hurt, when the man came to. He hoped it would.

He searched pockets until he found keys, and then went back up. Kendrick seemed to have got control of himself. He talked feverishly as Wales tried keys.

"There's still time before Doomsday, isn't there?" he pleaded. "Still time to get everybody off Earth? It isn't too late?"

"I think there may be time enough," Wales said. He got the shackles unlocked, and helped Kendrick to his feet. "But we've still Fairlie to reckon with."

Kendrick broke into raging curses, and Wales stopped him sharply. "Cut it, Lee. I feel exactly the same way about it but we've no time for hysteria. It'll be tricky trying to get to Fairlie in his own stronghold, over in New York. Tell me...has he come here often?"

"He hasn't been here for two weeks," Kendrick said. "He...and Bliss and the others in it with him...you know what they wanted of me? They wanted me to issue statements saying that Nereus might not hit Earth after all. They said they'd leave me here for Doomsday, if I didn't. Damn them—"

Again, Wales calmed him down. "Those guards didn't go over to New York to report to him, did they? Did they use radiophone?"

Kendrick looked startled. "Why, yes, they did. I've heard them. But I don't know what secret wavelength they used."

"Maybe," said Wales tightly, "we can find that out. Martha, you help him down the stairs. A few steps at a time, till his legs steady."

He hurried back down again. The wounded man he had tied up had recovered consciousness. He sat, his face a pallor of pain, and looked up at Wales with wide, fearful eyes.

"Yes," said Wales softly. "I'd love to kill you. You're right about that. But maybe I won't. What's your name?"

"Mowler."

"You know how to call Fairlie, on the portable radiophone? Well, you're going to call him. You're going to tell him just what I say."

By the time he found the radiophone and brought it, Kendrick was coming shakily down the last steps with Martha steadying him.

Wales asked Mowler, "What's the wave-length for Fairlie's private phone?"

Mowler, looking up into his face, shivered and told him. He set the dial.

Then he told the wounded man what to say. He finished, "Don't do it wrong."

Again looking into Wales' face, Mowler said, "I won't."

WALES TOUCHED the call button. He held the instrument in front of Mowler. And presently a voice came from it.

"Fairlie speaking."

"Mowler here," said Mowler.

"Our guest wants to see you. He says he's ready to make that statement now...any statement you want."

"About time," growled Fairlie's voice. "All right, I'll come."

Wales switched off the instrument and took it away. He went out on the parapet, and waited in the darkness with the Venn gun in his hands.

Martha and Kendrick came out, and as another Marslift ship flamed up across the sky, he saw that her face was white and strained.

She said, "Don't kill him, Jay."

He said, without turning. "The Evacuation has been delayed, and there may not be enough time to make up that delay. We may not get everyone off Earth in time. And every one of those who are left to face Doomsday will have been killed by Fairlie and his pals."

"I know," she said. "But don't, Jay."

He would make no promise, or answer. He waited. And they heard the purr of the fast power-boat, less than an hour later.

Dawn was gray in the eastern sky when Fairlie, and one armed man in Evacuation Police uniform, came up the steps to the pedestal.

Wales stepped out, the Venn gun leveled, and Kendrick came out behind him.

Fairlie stopped. The Police officer with him made an uncertain sound and movement.

"Don't be stupid," Fairlie said. "He's got us cold."

He came up a few more steps. He looked up at Wales, and there was in his powerful face an immense disgust.

"You're proud, aren't you, Wales?" said Fairlie. "You think you've done something big and gallant. You've saved, or tried to save, a lot of human lives and that makes you happy." He suddenly raged. "Human refuse! The weak, the unfit, the no-damned-good, that we've been saddled with all our lives here on Earth—and now we must take them with us to drag us all down on Mars."

"Don't, Jay," whispered Martha, and her voice was a painful sound.

Fairlie said:

"Let him. I'd sooner go out now as see all human civilization dragged down out there by the weight of the useless rabble who would be better dead."

Wales said, "You're so sure, just who should live and who should die. You felt such a big man, making secret decisions like that, didn't you? Fairlie, who knows what's best for everybody. You and your pals liked that feeling, didn't you? There have always been characters like you..."

He paused, and then he said, "We're going over to New York. We're going to have Kendrick tell his story to all the millions still on Earth, and it's a story that two of your own men will back up. We're going to try to get every last soul off Earth before Doomsday. But if we don't..."

"If you don't?" sneered Fairlie.

"You'll know it," said Wales, and now he was shaking. "Because you, Fairlie, will not leave Earth till every last soul is evacuated. If any human being faces Doomsday here, you'll face it right with him."

CHAPTER NINE

OVER NEW YORK there hung in the sky a new moon, big and red and terrifying.

Once it had been a mere track on an astronomical photo, a figure in a calculation. Once it had been a threat, but an abstract one. Now it was real at last. Week by week, it had grown from a spark to a speck to a little moon, and now Kendrick's World was rushing in fast toward the fatal rendezvous with its bigger, sister world.

Wales sat at his desk in the office high in the UN tower, and looked out the window at the skyscrapers looming strange in the bloody light. There was a great silence everywhere. The frantic thunder of the Marslift was stilled at last. The last-but-one rockets had left at dusk, and now as night advanced it seemed that the whole Earth was hushed and waiting.

He felt a weariness that smothered all happiness of success. For they *had* succeeded, in these four frantic months. After Lee Kendrick had told his story to the world, after the plotters who had ruthlessly condemned millions "for the good of the race" had been exposed and arrested, those millions of dubious folk had suddenly felt the full panicky shock of truth, had realized at last that Doomsday was real.

They had poured into New York, in fear-driven mobs that could hardly be handled. And Wales, as the hastily appointed new Evacuation Marshal, had felt in his soul that it was too late, that some would surely be left.

He had reckoned without that quality in human beings that draws their greatest strength out of peril. The Marslift had been speeded up, speeded up farther, speeded up until rocket-crews fainted of fatigue at their posts. But it had, at last, been done...

The door opened, and Martha came across the office to where Wales sat hunched and weary with his hands spread out on the empty desk.

"It's time, Jay," she said. "Lee and the others are waiting."

He looked slowly up at her. "We got them all off," he said.

"Yes. We got them all off."

"About one thing," he said, "Fairlie was right. It'll be hard on Mars for us, harder because of all those last millions. But I don't think anyone will ever complain."

He thought of the people who had streamed through New York, into the Marslift rockets, these last weeks and days.

He thought of Sam Lanterman and his people from Pittsburgh, and Lanterman complaining, "Hell, I got to own a whole city and what happens—I get scared out of it! Oh well, I guess it won't be so bad out there."

Martha touched his shoulder gently. "Come, Jay."

He got to his feet and walked heavily with her to the lift.

They went down through the silent, empty building to the empty street. Empty, except for the car in which Kendrick and the two others waited, looking up silently at the crimson face of the thing that was coming fast, fast, toward Earth.

The car bore them fast through the empty streets, and the lifeless metropolis fell behind them and they rushed across a countryside already wearing a strange and ominous new aspect, to the spaceport.

The last rocket waited, a silvery tower flashing back the red light from the sky. They got out of the car and walked toward it.

Hollenberg had won the honor of being the last rocket-captain to leave Earth. But he did not look as though he enjoyed that honor now.

"We're ready," he said.

Wales asked, "Is Fairlie aboard?"

Hollenberg nodded grimly. "Aboard, and locked up. He was the last evacuee taken on, as per orders."

They stood, looking at each other. It came to Wales what was the matter. They stood upon Earth, and it was the last time that they might ever stand upon it.

He said harshly, "If we're ready, let's go."

The rocket-ship bore them skyward on wings of flame and thunder, and an Earth empty of man lay waiting.

A MILLION MILES out in space, they watched from the observation port. They could see the planetoid only as a much smaller, dark mass against the blue, beautiful sphere of Earth.

"One minute, fifteen seconds," said Kendrick, in a dry, level voice.

Martha sobbed, and hid her face against Wales' shoulder, and he held her close.

"Thirty seconds."

And all Wales could think of was the cities and their silent streets, the little houses carefully locked and shuttered, the quiet country roads and old trees and fields, with the red moon looming over them, coming down upon them, closer, closer...

"She's struck," said Kendrick.

And then, "Look—look—"

Wales saw the blue sphere of Earth had suddenly changed—white steam laced with leaping flames enwrapped it, puffing out from it. Giant winds tore the steam and he glimpsed tortured continents buckling, cracking, mountains rising...

He held Martha close, and watched until he could watch no more, and turned away. Kendrick, with his telescope set up, was talking rapidly.

"The continental damage isn't too bad. The seas are all steam now, but they'll condense again in time. Terrific volcanoes, but they'll not last too long. In time, it'll cool down..."

In time, Wales thought. In their time? Maybe not until their children's time?

He looked ahead, at the red spark of Mars, the world of refuge. It would be hard living on Mars, yes, for all the millions of men. But there were other worlds in space, and they had the knowledge and the ships. He thought they would go farther than Mars, much farther. He thought that they could not guess now, how far.

But someday, they or their children would come back to old Earth again. Of that, he was very sure.

THE END

If you've enjoyed this book, you will not want to miss these terrific titles…

ARMCHAIR SCI-FI & HORROR DOUBLE NOVELS, $12.95 each

D-141   **ALL HEROES ARE HATED** by Milton Lesser
            AND THE STARS REMAIN by Bryan Berry

D-142   **LAST CALL FOR DOOMSDAY** by Edmond Hamilton
            HUNTRESS OF AKKAN by Robert Moore Williams

D-143   **THE MOON PIRATES** by Neil R. Jones
            CALLISTO AT WAR by Harl Vincent

D-144   **THUNDER IN THE DAWN** by Henry Kuttner
            THE UNCANNY EXPERIMENTS OF DR. VARSAG by David V. Reed

D-145   **A PATTERN FOR MONSTERS** by Randall Garrett
            STAR SURGEON by Alan E Nourse

D-146   **THE ATOM CURTAIN** by Nick Boddie Williams
            WARLOCK OF SHARRADOR by Gardner F. Fox

D-147   **SECRET OF THE LOST PLANET** by David Wright O'Brien
            TELEVISION HILL by George McLociard

D-148   **INTO THE GREEN PRISM** by A Hyatt Verrill
            WANDERERS OF THE WOLF-MOON by Nelson S. Bond

D-149   **MINIONS OF THE TIGER** by Chester S. Geier
            FOUNDING FATHER by J. F. Bone

D-150   **THE INVISIBLE MAN** by H. G. Wells
            THE ISLAND OF DR. MOREAU by H. G. Wells

ARMCHAIR SCIENCE FICTION CLASSICS, $12.95 each

C-61   **THE SHAVER MYSTERY, Book Six**
            by Richard. S. Shaver

C-62   **CADUCEUS WILD**
            by Ward Moore & Robert Bradford

ARMCHAIR MYSTERY-CRIME DOUBLE NOVELS, $12.95 each

B-1   **THE DEADLY PICK-UP** by Milton Ozaki
            KILLER TAKE ALL by James O. Causey

B-2   **THE VIOLENT ONES** by E. Howard Hunt
            HIGH HEEL HOMICIDE by Frederick C. Davis

B-3   **FURY ON SUNDAY** by Richard Matheson
            THE AGONY COLUMN by Earl Derr Biggers

STRANDED IN A LOST WORLD NOT OF THIS EARTH

King and Carson had come to the wilds of Upper Burma in search of their friend, Mackintosh, who had disappeared in the Burmese jungles many months earlier. When they found him, they heard bizarre tales of a lost temple and a mad high priest named Akbad. Even stranger, they heard Mackintosh rant on about an extraordinary place he'd visited, a place he could only describe as "heaven." But as wild as these accounts seemed, it wasn't long before King and Carson found themselves at the mercy of the of the very man Mackintosh had described as "a god." However, Akbad was a real man and a real high priest. Only his powers were far greater than anyone could have imagined, and before long King and Carson found themselves fighting for their lives in a horrifying world that had all the appearances of being another planet in another solar system…perhaps even in another universe! A planet ruled by a beautiful she-devil with a lust for blood.

CAST OF CHARACTERS

SANDY KING
As a former WWII fighter he was plenty tough, but in the jungles of Upper Burma there were things beyond the power of brawn.

AVENA
Her ability to hunt down and slay men proved that just because you're beautiful doesn't necessarily mean you're nice.

CAL CARSON
He was King's pal and willing to take a bullet for him—but a hot searing death from a glowing orb wasn't something he expected.

LEDA SORENSEN
When she and her father had vanished from the face of the Earth she found out what "fighting to survive" really meant.

AKBAD
His bizarre powers were like none possessed by any other human being—but was he really even human?

JAMES SORENSEN
He was a brilliant scientist and a learned professor, but he had vanished in the wilds of Upper Burma many years before.

SIN YUL
King had hired him because he was known to be a very good jungle guide. But when it came to loyalty?

THE HUNTRESS
OF AKKAN

By
ROBERT MOORE WILLIAMS

ARMCHAIR FICTION
PO Box 4369, Medford, Oregon 97504

*For more information about Armchair Books and products, visit our
website at…*

www.armchairfiction.com

Or email us at…

armchairfiction@yahoo.com

THE HUNTRESS OF AKKAN

Illustrated by JULIAN S. KRUPA

CHAPTER ONE

THE shrill yell split the hot night. Sandy King—late Captain Andrew King of the United States Army Intelligence Section in the Asiatic Theater of Operations— slid a swift hand under the rolled-up coat that was serving as a pillow and grabbed the handle of the automatic hidden there. The echoes of the yell—whether it came from beast, crazy man, or impossible creature of the night—had not stopped echoing through the half-wrecked Dak bungalow before he was fully awake. Men who had done the things he had done in the places he had done them either learned to awaken at the slightest sound or the time soon came when they did not awaken at all. King awakened instantly. The punkah fan on the ceiling had not stopped its last

THE HUNTRESS OF AKKAN

downward movement as the frightened coolie let go the pull rope before he was fully alert. He listened.

The even breathing of Cal Carson, late master sergeant attached to the intelligence section, faltered slightly, then continued as regularly as before. King knew that Carson was awake and ready, his gun half-drawn, but that the sergeant had no intention of letting a change in the tempo of his breathing reveal to a possible listener that he was awake. As good as they ever came, Carson.

At the other end of the room Sin Yul grunted and sat up, muttering a mixture of Burmese and Chinese curses under his breath, then abruptly was silent. King mentally cursed the guide, but after the initial movement, Sin Yul made no sound. Outside the half-wrecked Dak rest house there was silence.

Too much silence. The shrill of a night bird, the raucous mutter of one of the giant toads, the chipper-chip of a flying fox—they were really bats, big ones—would have been better than this stillness. Normally the jungle was never still, except of course when the tiger walked in the night.

It was no tiger that had screamed. Like their smaller brothers, the big cats preferred to keep quiet. Something else had howled—

"*Yooooowwww!*"

The sound came again, ripping a hole in the stillness, lifting the hair along the back of King's neck. Abruptly Sin Yul was shaking him.

"Welly wake up, Sahib. Bad no good monkey business heap go on outside. Sumpin' hollerin' there, Sahib King, sair—"

"Shut up..."

Hissing with indrawn breath, Sin Yul relapsed into flustered silence. King rose, slipped on his boots, slid to the jagged hole that served as a window. As he moved he was aware that Carson had already slipped on his boots and was coming with him. They looked out.

In front of the bungalow was a little clearing. Their bearer coolies had built a tiny blaze in the open space and had been huddled around it. At the first yell the coolies had silently decamped. Beyond the clearing the bamboo began, the thick, heavy bamboo of the rain forests of Upper Burma. Mile upon mile of the green plants stretched down the side of the mountain.

Light from a three-quarter waxing moon poured into the clearing, revealing nothing.

"It's in the bamboo," Carson whispered.

"Yeah."

"What the devil do you think it is, Sandy?"

"An owl, maybe?"

"Yeah? Sandy, I've heard an owl or two in my time, and I never heard no owl make a sound like that."

"Neither have I," said King dryly.

They waited. Silence held the bamboo forest. Behind them, Sin Yul's heavy breathing was audible.

"I can slip out the back and make a circle in that bamboo and flush him out and you can pot him when he shows," Carson suggested.

"You stay here," King abruptly ordered. "A fat chance you'd have out there in that bamboo."

"I flushed me some of our little Japanese brothers out of some bamboo once, and you potted 'em as they came out," Carson pointed out.

"I know. But that's something else out there now. *Shhh! There it is!*"

AGAINST the dark blotch of the bamboo a shadow had moved. It was just a shadow, a movement in darkness, barely discernible. Every sense alert, King watched. Something was standing there at the edge of the clearing, watching the bungalow. Was it—the fleeting thought flashed through King's mind—was it watching them? Did it know they were in the rest house? Had it come here seeking them?

He shrugged the thought aside. Whatever crouched out there in the darkness, it could not have come looking for them. For if it was after them, then their reason for being here was known.

That was impossible. No one but he and Carson knew why they were here, what monstrous secret they sought here in these tortuous mountains of Upper Burma. He and Carson and Mackintosh, if he was still alive, did not, could not, know they were here. No, the thing out there in the darkness was not seeking them. Its presence out there was due to accident, nothing else. He hoped.

It came out of the darkness. It darted toward the bungalow, stopped halfway, stood looking fearfully, hesitantly toward the ruined rest house.

"It's a man..." Carson whispered.

It was a man, but it had run half-bent over like an animal. Now it stood erect, leaning forward, looking toward the bungalow. A man. A thin, gaunt skeleton of man, naked except for a ragged strip of cloth around his middle. Bearded, with long, tangled hair. A scarecrow and a skeleton.

"If ever I saw the walking picture of starvation... Hey, it's coming in."

A twig had snapped in the thick bamboo. At the sound, the man had turned his head with the quick motion of a startled animal. For a split second he had listened, his head cocked at an angle. Then he turned and darted toward the bungalow.

"Mackintosh!" King suddenly yelled. "In here, man, in here. We'll cover you."

In spite of the absence of clothing, in spite of the gaunt frame, he had recognized this scarecrow. Mackintosh! The man they had come here seeking. Their friend, their more than friend, their buddy. Their sharer of a thousand dangers, Mackintosh, late—although he probably didn't know that the war with Japan had ended and his connection with the service had terminated—late of the United States Army Intelligence Corps. The quick way he had turned his head, the cock of his chin as he listened, by these two characteristics alone King would have recognized Mackintosh among thousands.

This was Mackintosh!

He stopped instantly, stared toward the bungalow.

"Sandy! Is it you I'm hearin' or am I still in Heaven?"

"Mack, it's me all right. Mack, *look out!*"

OUT of the dark bamboo forest four figures had hurtled. Like dogs on the scent of prey, they leaped straight toward Mackintosh! The pistol in King's hand jutted fire. He shot without taking aim but at the explosive blast of the pistol, the foremost shadow leaping from the forest collapsed in a huddle and sprawled forward, the knife blade in his hand glinting in the moonlight. The second figure stumbled over the fallen man and King's bullet went over his head. The other two darted back into the bamboo, followed immediately by the other.

"Sandy! Man, am I glad to see you!" Mackintosh's hand was lean and bony and wet. "And Cal. This is like old home week, isn't it? Mind if I sit down?"

King could feel Mackintosh sagging. "Whiskey!" he said to Sin Yul, and the Chinaman scurried among their supplies as he obeyed. Mackintosh sat down on the floor, half in, half out of the moonlight pouring through the broken window where Carson had already resumed his guard position.

"We got your message," King said.

"Ah. I wondered if it would be delivered—ah—in time."

"In time?"

"In time to do me any good. I didn't doubt that you would come hot-footing it up here as soon as you could get leave but I did doubt if the old man would let you come—"

"Paying attention to generals went out of fashion when the war ended," King grunted.

"Man, you mean the war's over?" Mackintosh shouted. "You mean the lads have hung Tojo on a sour cherry tree and marched down the streets of Tokyo?"

"That they have," King answered. "The Japanese fleet is at the bottom of the sea and the warlords are in hell where they belong."

"Well, now that is what I call good news," Mackintosh said, satisfaction in his voice. "Yes, indeed. They got what was coming to them. That listens mighty fine. Many a time we looked forward to the day when the war would end and we would go marching home, eh Sandy? To think it's finally come…"

King let him talk. A man who had fought through the war had a right to let off a little steam when he first learned that the fighting was over. Mackintosh seemed a little dazed at the news. King gently steered him to another subject.

"That yell? Eh, Sandy, I forgot you didn't know about it. The lads out there..." He waved his hand toward the window where Carson crouched on guard. "...the lads out there were doing the yelling. Havin' fun, they were."

"Fun?"

"Yeah. *They* thought it was fun," Mackintosh drawled. "Thanks, Gunga Din. I'll have another drop of that whiskey, if you don't mind." The liquor slopped from the aluminum cup as he lifted it to his lips. He seemed to find strength in the drink. "Playin' a game, they were. Yeah...a game."

"Um. Who are they?"

"WHO are they? Well, now that's a question. The army classification section would classify them as assassins, skilled, which would be understating their ability in the fine art of murder. We thought the commando schools taught us something about killing, but, Sandy, we're just amateurs compared to those lads..."

"Who are they?" King grunted.

"Yes, yes. I was wanderin' from the subject, wasn't I? They work for Akbad. And Akbad—" The voice trailed into silence.

"Go on," King gently prodded. "Who is Akbad? You never mentioned him in your message."

"I'm trying to think of some way to tell you who Akbad is," Mackintosh thoughtfully continued. "Akbad is a man. He's a Chinese or a Hindu or a Mongol or a Burmese, or a cross between any of these and any other Asiatic race you can mention. But he's a man all right. I'm pretty sure about that. Or at least I *think* he's a man—"

King felt a little sliver of cold run up his spine as if a spider with tiny, ice-cold feet had run up his back. Had Mack blown his top? Had danger and exhaustion and fatigue taken their deadly toll?

"What the hell, Mack?"

As if he had not heard him, Mackintosh continued, "Akbad is the high priest of a certain temple located near here, the *Temple of the Forbidden Delight,* I believe they call it, in their squishy language. It's an old temple, older than the hills, older than Burma, older than China, maybe older than the human race for all I know. There were times when I wondered how old it was. Ah…wandering again. Akbad is the big shot of this temple. Sandy, there were times when I thought he was a man, and times when I didn't know what he was. When I didn't know what he was, Sandy, those were the times when I thought he was a god."

"What?"

"Still think it, too" Mackintosh stubbornly insisted. "No, don't look toward that medicine kit. I don't need any atabrine or quinine. But if you want to think I'm out of my head, I'm willing to agree with you, because Sandy, either my eyes are liars, or I have seen the impossible happen."

KING pulled a package of cigarettes out of his pocket, started to light one, remembered where he was, and thrust both cigarette and match back where he had got them.

"Like what?" he said cautiously.

"Um? Oh. Well, I've seen men vanish."

"I've seen elephants vanish, on the stage."

"This wasn't on the stage."

King was silent.

"Matter of fact, I've vanished myself," Mackintosh continued.

"Yes."

"Matter of fact, I've been to heaven."

"Uh!"

"I've seen the pearly gates, Sandy, glittering in the sky. Oh, I didn't get up close enough to touch 'em, but I saw 'em. And I saw angels flying through the air and I heard the harper's chorus playing before the throne—"

"Skip it!"

"Huh?"

"Start over, at the beginning, and come again, Mack. And this time, lad, don't tell me your hashish dreams or I'll clip you on the conk."

"Well, maybe they were dreams, but I don't think—"

"Start at the beginning..."

"All right. All right. You sound like a blasted colonel!" For a moment irritation showed in his voice. Then Mackintosh continued, "As you know, I came up here looking for a secret radio station that our little Japanese brothers had hidden somewhere back in these hills. Didn't find the damned thing—"

"The Air Force found it," King interrupted. "After that, it wasn't there anymore."

"So that was why it went off the air. Stout fellas, those Air Force lads. Well, when I couldn't pick it up anymore and hence couldn't get a directional fix on it with the little receiver I had, I thought the Japanese had gotten wise and moved it. So, I started back. Trouble was, I took a short cut."

"Yes?"

"Bad mistake, that short cut. Got off the beaten track. Got lost as hell. Wandered into Akbad's territory by mistake. Matter of fact, I wandered right straight into his temple. And that, Sandy, was wrong."

"So I gather. These natives are likely to be touchy as hell about their temples. What happened?"

"I was fed the fatted calf. Wine, the very best, better food than I had seen in two years. A private harem for my very own. Little beauties all lined up in front of me and I was given my choice of all or any. I was bathed, rubbed with ointments, perfumed, given the softest robes you can imagine. Anything you can think of, I had it for the asking. They really had the welcome sign out on the doormat."

"Sounds like quite a place."

"It was. It is…"

"What was wrong with it?"

"That is what I don't know."

"But—"

"If I knew what happened to me, really knew what actually took place, then maybe I could tell you what was wrong."

"What do you think happened to you? Mack, darn your hide…get specific. What were they doing? Fattening you up to sacrifice you?"

"Sacrifice me?" Mackintosh shrugged. "Oh, no—nothing like that. They were fattening me up so I would be in the proper shape to go…ah…to heaven…"

"Mack!"

"They were going to send me there. Fact is, they did send me there. Fact is—"

AT THE window, Carson grunted. A gun thundered. King turned. Flickering past his eyes, darting in through the broken window, was a billiard ball that glowed with a milky whiteness. Carson fired one shot at it, missed. For a split second, it hung in the air. In that second there ripped from Mackintosh's throat such a scream as King had never heard come from a human being. It was the scream of a man who has been tortured, goaded long past the breaking point, and who, knowing that the last terrible moment is upon him, spends the last remnants of his strength in one soul-wrenching yell.

Mackintosh leaped to his feet, dived toward the window on the opposite side of the room. The ball hesitated for a second, then darted after him, leaped at him, chased him, overtook him, seemed to touch him, to rest for a moment on his skin. Then it passed from sight.

For an instant, King could not see it. In that split second, Mackintosh screamed again, a sound that died swiftly into a gurgle. As the scream died, Mackintosh began to fall. As he fell, the billiard ball reappeared. It was on the other side of him. It leaped up into the air almost to the ceiling, hung there. For a moment it was filmed with a reddish mist. Then the redness faded and its surface was again milky white.

Mackintosh was falling. He still retained the momentum gained in the mad dash for the farther window. It kept him moving. But his legs would no longer support him and as he moved, he fell. He hit the wall with a crunch, sagged to the floor, and did not move.

The billiard ball darted down, hovered over him, then rose into the air and flitted out the window.

King pulled a flashlight out of his pocket, moved forward, bent down, shielded the rays, and turned the beam on Mackintosh. He turned off the light, straightened up. Sin Yul's frightened eyes were on him. From the window Carson watched him. He wiped sudden drops of sweat from his face.

Mackintosh was dead. A hole had been burned completely through his body. The hole was exactly as big and exactly as round as a billiard ball.

CHAPTER TWO

KING stood in the middle of the floor, not moving, not thinking, not letting himself think. He could hear Sin Yul breathing heavily, like a horse with asthma. At the window, Carson had not moved.

Mack was dead. That was not possible. *Mack was dead.* A billiard ball that flew through the air had burned a hole through him and then had floated out the window. Somewhere near here was a temple ruled by a man named Akbad, except that maybe Akbad wasn't a man. Then what the hell was he? Skin crawled all over King's body.

"Yoooowwww!"

The screech echoed through the night outside, rolled across the bamboo forest, lifting King's hair, speeding up the pounding of his already racing heart.

"They're comin', Sandy," Carson whispered.

King stepped to the window. Dark figures were moving out of the bamboo. Carson's gun covered them but Carson did not shoot. They made no effort at concealment. King saw why.

The billiard ball was dancing in the air before them. Like a playful firefly, it was darting, dancing, twisting ahead of them, leading them straight toward the wrecked bungalow.

"I can mow 'em down," Carson whispered.

"But can you mow *it* down?" King answered.

Could either of them hit the dancing ball? And if they did hit it, would a slug from a pistol harm it?

"Sandy, we got to do one or the other damned quick," Carson said.

"I know, Cal. Fight or give up?"

"Wait here," King said.

He stepped outside. The ball leaped up to treetop level, danced there a second as if surprised, began to move in quick, eccentric circles, darted forward, drew back, was never still for a moment. The men had stopped. Out of the corners of their eyes they watched the ball as if they were waiting for orders from it. There were four of them, bearded, with close-cropped hair, except for sandals and loincloths, naked. In the moonlight King could see them clearly. Their faces were the faces of Caucasians, thin noses, high foreheads, but their skin was Negro black. Each carried a hooked knife in his hand, had another like it stuck into his belt.

"Well?" said King.

The four men did not move. The ball danced above them. The night was silent. King could hear his heart pounding, could feel the throb of his pulse at his temple. The silence held. Sweat ran down over King's eyelids and into his eyes. He dared not brush it away.

"Well?" he repeated.

"Bravo!" a voice answered from far away. "A stout fella. A stout fella, indeed!" There was a soft sound like the clapping of hands and it too was far away.

"Who spoke?" King whispered.

Laughter answered him.

"Who spoke?" he rasped.

"I spoke," the faraway voice answered. "I, Akbad—"

"You—"

"You seem to recognize my name..."

"Where are you?"

"Where does the brave one think I am?"

"I don't know. Where are you?"

Laughter sounded far away. "You seem disturbed, my brave one." The words were slurred, almost a hiss. "You shall soon know where I am. You shall soon know. Ha! Or do you want to try to use that gun you are clutching so nervously? Do you wish to signal your brave companions hiding inside the building to shoot too? Perhaps you would prefer to do that, no?"

"I *could* do that," King said.

AS HE spoke, he was aware that the glittering ball, darting in circles above him, seemed suddenly to poise itself as if it was getting ready to dart toward him. A lion, in that split second before the charge, acted like that. He remembered Mackintosh and how the ball had overtaken him when he tried to run, how it had slid through him like a red-hot ball bearing diving into a tub of butter.

"Do you wish to shoot?" the far-off voice anxiously inquired. There was eagerness in that voice. King heard the eagerness. And realized that Akbad wanted him to shoot, wanted him to resist. Mackintosh had said the lads had been playing a game, had been having fun. No doubt Akbad, wherever he was, had been participating in that game. Rearing the eagerness in the far-off voice, King realized how hellish that game was.

"You win, Akbad," King said. "There will be no shooting, tonight." He tossed his pistol on the ground in front of him. "See...I offer no resistance. Carson! Sin Yul! Lay down your guns and come out here. There will be no shooting tonight, Akbad."

"Some other night, perhaps?" the far-off voice regretfully said. "Ah, well, if that is what you wish, then that is the way it must be. The wishes of my guests are sacred and you are now my guest. My servants will show you what to do. Eknar el h'singto!"

The last words were in a foreign tongue. The four men leaped to obey. By signs they directed that the three men were to follow them. They led them up a trail into the bamboo forest along the edge of the mountain.

"What makes, Sandy?" Carson inquired.

"Lord, Cal, I wish I knew," King fervently answered. "The same thing that caught Mack has caught us." He glanced up. Flitting along above the trail, following them just above the level of the treetops, was the softly glowing billiard ball.

"Maybe we should have fought it out back there," King muttered.

"We were dead men if we did," Cal Carson answered.

"Wish make suggest we are all-same dead men anyhow!" Sin Yul blurted out, breaking his silence for the first time.

THE temple of Akbad lay well up in the hills, in the rocky cleft of a mountain peak that a squad of men could defend against an army. They climbed all night to reach it, two of the natives ahead leading the way, two bringing up the rear as guards. The ball floated overhead, following them like some tiny but extremely vicious watchdog. Dawn was lighting the mountain peaks when they reached the temple. It squatted in the monstrous cliffs like some hideous toad, fat-bellied and warty, poisonous. And it was old, as old as mountains around it. The huge granite blocks that made up its outer walls were weathered smooth. Not in a year or in a thousand years would tough granite weather to such crumbling smoothness. The individual building blocks were huge, weighing tons. King had seen the granite blocks that went into the Egyptian pyramids, the single gigantic chunk of stone that lies in the quarry outside ruined Baalbek, stones so big that modern engineers do not even now understand how they were moved. The blocks in this temple were larger. It looked older than the pyramids, older than Baalbek, older than Nineveh, older than the Biblical cities of the plains of ancient Abraham.

An old, old temple shaped like a toad hugging a mountain cleft in Upper Burma. The two natives running ahead of them, the ball following above, they trudged toward the gate, were taken inside, into a room as richly and as grotesquely furnished as any King had ever seen. No storied sultan of India, no Maharajah, had softer rugs than these on his palace floors, had tapestries worked with so much gold thread, encrusted with so many gems, on his walls.

And no king, no sultan, no khan, no czar, ever had a picture like this to hang on his walls.

It was the picture of a girl, of a young woman. She was sitting easily in a carved antique chair of a design that was carried out in the priceless diadem pushed high up on her head. At her breast, held on a chain that circled her throat, was a single glittering jewel so cleverly painted that it seemed to give off gleams of sparkling white light.

She was the most beautiful woman King had ever seen. Looking at her, he felt a sudden pulse of blood in his heart. This was the girl he had been searching for, ever since he was twenty. He had looked for her all over the world, always hoping that somehow, around the next turning of the road, across from him at the next dinner party he attended, he would find her. He hadn't found her, but he had found her picture, painted, if he was any judge, by a better artist than had ever existed on Earth. Da Vinci had not done better than this. Raphael, Van Dyke, Petty, Varga—they could all take lessons from this artist, this completely unknown perfect painter of perfect women.

THERE were other pictures to be seen. The walls, even the ceiling, were covered with them. King did not like them.

They were hunting scenes, every one of them. Here, in heavy jungle, grotesque little men were stalking a tiger. Armed with spears, another group was facing the charge of a lion. A third painting revealed a strange beast that King did not recognize.

"By the Lord Harry, that's a saber tooth tiger!" someone grunted.

It was Cal Carson who had spoken. Carson had also been looking at the paintings.

"I was in the Field Museum in Chicago once," Carson said. "They had some pictures of animals that once lived on Earth. This was one of them."

"Sure you're not mistaken?"

"Not a chance. You couldn't be wrong about those fangs. But how—" His voice faded into silence.

"How what?" King asked.

"I was wondering," Carson hesitantly answered. "The Museum scientists had found the bones of the saber-tooth tiger. Then they had figured out how he would look and the artist had drawn the picture. But—"

"I know," King interrupted. "I was thinking the same thing. There haven't been any saber-tooth tigers on Earth for ten, twenty, maybe fifty thousand years. How did the guy who drew *these* pictures know that such a beast ever existed?"

"Do you suppose the fellow who drew these pictures actually *saw* a saber tooth tiger?" Carson questioned.

King said nothing. There were other pictures. He liked these least of all. They were still hunting scenes but the prey that was being hunted was—men. The same grotesque little men in the flowing robes were the hunters. Their weapons were the same. But they were hunting men.

A race of hunters, King thought. The people who drew these pictures had but one aim in life—to hunt.

Clicking, the door of the room opened. King whirled. Slaves entered. Carrying pitchers of steaming water, they removed a screen at one end of the room, revealed a bathtub carved out of a single piece of marble. By signs, they indicated they had come to bathe the three men. King shrugged, stepped forward, slipped out of his clothes. They were bathed, given clean, fresh clothes, allowed to rest. Then other slaves entered. They carried food. Delicate venison, bowls of fruit, a pleasant red wine. They ate until they could hold no more.

"It's food for a king," Cal Carson sighed. "But somehow I'd trade all of it for a couple of hamburgers with onions and some French fries. Sandy, what the hell have we got into anyhow?"

BEFORE King could attempt to answer, the door opened again. Six girls entered. They were shapely wenches, a little on the darkish side so far as complexion went, but shapely. King's jaw dropped when he realized why they had come.

"And I thought Mac was having hallucinations!" he gulped.

Carson looked sheepish. Sin Yul sat up, a sudden glitter appearing in his dark eyes at the sight of the women.

"Beat it!" King growled, waving toward the door.

Startled looks appeared on the faces of the girls. They did not understand the words but the gesture toward the door they did understand. They hesitated.

"Scram!" King yelled, pointing again to the door.

The girls, like frightened rabbits, scampered out of the room. King faced the rather regretful gaze of Carson and the hot glare of Sin Yul.

"Girls, by damn! Why send away?" Sin Yul demanded.

"I want to see Akbad, not sluts," King said flatly.

"Permission granted," a voice spoke from somewhere in the room.

King jerked around, seeking the source of the voice. Carson had risen to his feet. Sin Yul was crouched, his right hand digging at his girdle for the dagger that was not there.

The room was empty. When the voice spoke, the slaves who had brought in the food, dashed madly for the door. Strong sunlight streamed through the eastern window.

"There's a loudspeaker hidden here," King muttered.

"No," the voice contradicted. "I am here, in the room with you."

"What?"

"You would like to see me, no? Very well. Watch."

In the middle of the room, directly in the bright sunlight, was a sudden flurry of fluorescing lights, purples, and violets. For a second they flared too brightly to watch. Then they were gone. In the spot where the lights had formed, a man stood.

He was tall, six feet six inches at least. And very thin. Skin the color of a green lemon was taut over a narrow, cameo-like face. A small narrow mouth; shoe-button-black, tired, sated, dissipated eyes.

"I am Akbad!" he said.

CHAPTER THREE

"IT'S a good trick," King bluntly said.

"You refer to my sudden appearance?" Akbad answered. "I agree. It is a good trick. And I *can* do it."

"You can at that," King agreed. "But I still think it's a trick."

Akbad spread his hands. "Did I say it wasn't? But can you do it?"

"Well, no," King answered. "But I would like to learn. Mind telling me how you work it?"

Akbad's face spread into a smile. "Really, now, even a guest can ask too much."

"Guests? Are we guests?"

"But of course you are my guests, for the time being."

"Hmmm," King mused. "Guests? Would you mind telling us what privileges we have as…ah…guests?"

"Delighted to tell you," Akbad answered. He waved his hands expansively and for a moment he looked like some far-fetched war millionaire showing off the treasures of his estate. "My guests get everything. While they remain with me, they have the best food obtainable in this wretched land, luxurious surroundings in which to live, beautiful paintings to stimulate the senses, every delight that ingenuity can create."

"Everything we want, we get?"

"Everything. Girls—"

"Including the privilege of walking out the front gate?" King interrupted.

"Of course!" Akbad said. "Nothing would delight me more. However..." Regret showed in his voice. "...it is my duty to warn you: there are certain dangers surrounding this castle and you might find a long journey would be a little on the difficult side. However, if you really want to leave me, it is your privilege. The man who was here—what was his name, now? For the moment it escapes me. Mackintosh. That was it. He chose the privilege of leaving my castle. Of course he went surreptitiously, at night, in a way that he thought was safe. I believe he eventually discovered his error."

"Yes," King said grimly. "I believe Mack knew he had made a mistake, though he didn't admit it."

"He was not the admitting kind," Akbad said. "If I must say it, he was a most unreasonable person, not satisfied with anything we could do for him. We did everything to please him but still he was not satisfied. He was what you call a Yankee. Perhaps that explains it. The other Yankees were also difficult."

"You have had others?"

"A few," Akbad admitted. "Frankly, we are making plans to secure more of them, many more. We have found them admirably suited to our purposes. They are great players of the great game—"

"The great game?" King interrupted.

"Yes."

"What the hell is that?"

Akbad bowed. "In time you will find out," he answered.

Where he was standing, purple and violet lights fluoresced in a glow of blinding light. For a second the glow held. Then it disappeared. Akbad was gone.

King listened, watched closely. There was no sign of movement in the room, no whisper of movement. Somewhere behind one of the tapestries a door clicked softly. That was all.

Akbad was gone.

"SANDY, I don't like it," Carson said. "I'm going to see if maybe there isn't some way out of here."

While King watched, Carson began a slow, methodical search of the walls. King laid down, made no effort to help. Escaping from the room where they were held would not solve their problem nor even begin to solve it. Was there any solution, he wondered, trying to recall the tales he had heard of this country. In the two years he had spent in Burma he had heard many stories, most of them too fantastic to credit. There was supposed to be an enchanted palace somewhere in these mountains, the natives said. Tigers with wings hid in the bamboo thickets. The natives, of course, were natural liars; but after all, this was Burma. Thugee was still a cult here. In this land—and the records proved it—was a clan who made a practice of committing murder. Civilizations had flourished here while Europe was a wilderness and America was inhabited only by roving nomads. It was an old land, and all old lands have their memories of evil, memories too often founded in grim fact.

King tried to remember what he had heard. There was a story of a Professor Sorenson, a scientist of some kind, who had come to Upper Burma about five years before the war started. He had told the British authorities that he was an ethnologist and they had given him permission to go where he pleased. Somewhere up in this section, he had vanished. Then there were a few American airmen, forced down by engine failure in this land. Some of them had radioed that they were going down; few of them had ever come out. What had happened to the ones who had vanished? A B-29 had gone down up here. No member of its crew had ever reported in. Nor had an extensive search revealed what had happened to them.

Mackintosh—King remembered the note the ragged, exhausted native had slipped into his hands. A note from Mack, saying he had run into something big. Mack had hinted at rooms piled full of jewels and if King could make it up there, both of them would be rich. Mack had said that he was being held as a kind of prisoner, but he had hinted he thought he could escape but didn't want to escape until he had solved some mystery.

Mack hadn't said what the mystery was. He hadn't known. He was going to do some more looking around. "It's big, Sandy; so damned big I don't want to talk about it. But will you please get up here if you possibly can."

Mack was dead back there in a dark bungalow, a hole burned through him.

KING resolutely forced himself not to think of the way Mack had died. That cursed floating billiard ball—what was it? Akbad controlled it; but what was it? Was it some kind of a mechanical device containing a microscopic but very powerful radio receiver and transmitter? Did it eject some kind of a ray, some burning beam that seared through human flesh? Or was it...a living creature, a horror out of some hell? He did not know. Nor did he know what Mackintosh had been talking about when he had said the thugs who were chasing him were playing a game. What sort of a game was it that had death as its object?

And Akbad—who was he? Mackintosh had had a great many doubts about Akbad. Mack had not even been certain that Akbad was human. Where had he learned to speak English? And if he wasn't human, what was he? King's mind was going round and round. Akbad's vanishing was startling but not terrifying. King knew that at least a scientific theory of a means of controlling invisibility had been worked out by scientists of the Western world. Here, in the Eastern world, it was perhaps possible that unknown scientists had gone from theory to fact, had succeeded in creating a cloak of invisibility. But...always the doubt remained. What was Akbad? Was he human or was he—something else?

King was tired, so tired he could barely think. To meet the dangers he grimly suspected lay ahead of them, he would need rest, all of it he could get. Forcing his mind to relax, he went to sleep.

He awakened with a start. Somewhere a drum was beating. He could hear the rhythmic pulsation through the door of the room. The sound was growing louder.

A dim radiance streamed through the windows of the room. He had slept the whole day through. Night had fallen. In the shadowed darkness he could hear Carson and Sin Yul stirring.

"Hear that, Sandy?" Carson whispered.

King nodded. His hand went to his hip feeling for the gun that was not there. The drum came nearer. The door opened.

Into the room, dancing, gyrating, pulsating with its milky radiance, came the billiard ball. It darted upward, took up a position near the ceiling, and continued its erratic dance.

Following it through the door came eight guards, with drawn knives.

King heard Carson grunt, heard Sin Yul hiss with fear. He rose slowly to his feet.

"Well?"

Akbad's voice came from far away.

"Follow where the guards take you."

TWO of the naked, black-skinned men took up the position of guides. The others fell in behind. By signs they indicated that King, Carson, and Sin Yul were to fall in between the two groups. King did not move. He stood in the middle of the room, hands on hips.

"Ah!" said Akbad. There was no mistaking the voice but there was also no way to determine its source. One thing was certain: Akbad knew every move they made, or did not make. He might be in the room; he might be somewhere else. It was certain he was watching them.

"Where are we going?" King said.

"To play the great game."

"What is that?"

Akbad laughed. There was no mirth in the sound. "In time, you will learn."

"What if we don't choose to learn?"

Akbad, as though a little surprised, hesitated. "In that case—but you don't have any choice."

"We always have a choice," King said grimly.

Akbad seemed to consider. "Yes, that is true," he admitted at last. "H'ai tang!" The last, in the foreign tongue, was spoken to the guards.

In the shadowed darkness King could not be quite certain how the guards reacted to whatever it was Akbad had said to them. They didn't move but he was aware of two things: that their eyes were fixed intently on him, and that they seemed to have stopped breathing.

He knew the signs.

"Do you insist on choosing?" Akbad questioned.

King sighed. "In the face of such persuasiveness, what can we do except obey?"

Motioning to Carson and Sin Yul to do likewise, he stepped into the place the guards had indicated. They seemed disappointed. "Some other time," he said, "you can use those knives."

The two guides started walking.

King and his two companions followed. The trail led through a gigantic room that had apparently at one time been a banquet hall, across a courtyard open to the sky above, where he caught a glimpse of the mountain towering over them. Then they were led into a squat, round fortress set against the base of the cliff that towered overhead. Here other guards hastily opened a door. They entered a tunnel. Their guides procured torches, motioned them to follow.

Behind them, twisting, gyrating, turning, came the billiard ball. It seemed to watch every move they made. King did not have to guess what would happen if they made a sudden dash for freedom.

The ball would follow them. As it had followed Mackintosh!

Walking was becoming difficult.

AN INVISIBLE wind blowing down the tunnel seemed to be pushing against them. He had to lean forward to make any progress. The guards, Carson, Sin Yul, were similarly affected.

"What the hell is making walking so hard?" Carson questioned.

"Don't know," King muttered.

The tunnel they were in seemed to follow the lines of an ancient cave. In places the walls had been dug away; in other places stone bridges had been erected over chasms. The boots of the Americans rang hollowly on the stone bridges. They crossed a chasm that seemed to lead down into the uttermost depths of the earth.

The invisible wind was blowing stronger. The guards were bent half over against it.

It wasn't a wind. There was no discernible movement of air. It was a pressure, a growing pressure, like the force of an accelerating body of air.

A wind that wasn't blowing a wind. King could feel depths of chill creeping through his body. Where were these guards taking them? What kind of a game was played here in the heart of this mountain?

They came to a round chamber. The guides stopped. Holding their torches as high as they could reach, they motioned for King and his companions to step forward.

The invisible wind was strongest here. It seemed to have its source here in this round chamber in the heart of the mountain. Gingerly, very slowly, King stepped forward.

The pressure was so strong he could barely move against it. It pulsed through his body, seemed to reach every molecule of his being, a torrent of invisible wind. He leaned forward, kept leaning forward. At this angle, he should fall. He didn't fall. The invisible wind buoyed him up, lifted him, kept him from falling. Sin Yul and Carson followed slowly behind him.

The guards remained at the entrance, not entering the round chamber.

The cave, cavern, chamber, hole, whatever it was—was in solid granite. Apparently some titanic convulsion of the earth in long gone ages had created a bubble here. When this granite was cooling lava in a gigantic earth cistern a gas bubble had formed this round chamber. The granite had cooled; the chamber had remained.

A chamber through which flowed a torrent of invisible wind.

"Goodbye," Akbad whispered, far away.

The pressure grew stronger. For an instant King had the impression that mad winds were howling savagely around him. The winds seemed to pick him up, to toss him as a straw is tossed by a hurricane. He was lifted, thrown, tossed in a dozen directions at once.

His last impression was that he was falling.

Like a light that is turned off, consciousness faded out.

CHAPTER FOUR

"BETTER get movin', Bub," the voice said. It was a tired voice, not much interested in what it was saying. King listened. He did not open his eyes. He was not sure he had the strength to open them. He was not at all certain he wanted to see what opening his eyes would reveal. Thousands of little pains that felt like microscopic red-hot needles jabbing him were running through his body. He felt as if he had been wrenched, that every muscle and bone in his body had been turned in the wrong direction and then had been inexpertly returned to their proper positions. He lay very still wondering how a man who hurt as much as he did could possibly be alive. The pain that swept through him was the granddaddy of all aches. It was spelled with a capital "P." It was the biggest pain that had ever existed.

The tired voice spoke again. "Better get movin', boys," it said.

Still he did not move.

A second voice spoke. It was a quick voice, speaking with the rapidity of a chirping bird.

"Maybe they're dead," it said. It spoke so rapidly that all the words ran together.

King didn't move. If he was dead he wouldn't much care. What had happened to him? He tried to remember. His mind was foggy. Vaguely he recalled a man named Akbad who had talked about playing some kind of a game.

Near him someone sighed. The sigh turned into a groan.

"If they're not dead, they soon will be," the tired voice observed.

Experimentally, King moved an arm. To his surprise, the arm moved. He thought about that.

"I saw one of them move!" the rapid bird voice excitedly chirped. "They're alive. We ought to get 'em out of there!"

"Why?" the tired voice reasonably asked. "If they die there, they won't have to try to stay alive in this damned country. Besides, I'm tired."

"We oughta get 'em out," the rapid bird voice stubbornly insisted.

"*You* get 'em out," the tired voice said. "*You* go down there and carry them up."

The bird voice was silent.

SANDY KING lay still. He had discovered a new fact, something that felt a little like the pressure of running water and a little more like the blast of wind from the prop of a P-47 was running or blowing over him. It was pushing against him, nudging him, trying to shove him. He thought about this water or wind. Somehow he didn't like it.

Near him he was vaguely aware someone was whispering rapidly in a mixture of languages that sounded like Chinese, Burmese, and Japanese. The groan came again. He thought about moving, about opening his eyes. Either one was simply too much effort.

"What's happening here?" a third voice spoke. It was a woman's voice and it was as sharp as a whip. Plainer than words, it said that the speaker had already seen what was going on and didn't like it in the least.

The shock of hearing a woman speak forced King to open his eyes. He shut them again almost instantly. The sunlight blinded him. In the one glance he saw that he was in a cup-like depression apparently carved out of solid rock. Standing on the edge of the depression, looking down at him, were two ragged, bearded men. Behind the men were trees. The third person on the edge of the depression was a girl.

"Why didn't you get them out of there?" she was demanding. The men, looking shamefaced, were starting down the edges of the cup. The girl was ahead of them. Wearing sandals, her only garment made out of animal skins, she came down the sloping edge of the cup with the lithe agility of a deer.

King tried to get to his feet. He succeeded only in sitting up. The girl bent over him. She had blue eyes and smooth brown skin and freckles on her nose.

"How do you feel?" she said.

"Better, now that I've seen you." He wiped sweat from his forehead. "Would you—ah mind—I'm a little vague. But, where am I? And what happened? I have hazy memories... Oh, hello, Cal. Were you doing that groaning?"

FOR the first time he noticed his two companions were still with him. Carson was getting groggily to his feet. Sin Yul, blinking his eyes, was trying to crawl toward the edge of the cup.

"I was doin' the groanin'," Carson answered. "Feel like doin' some more of it." His eyes went around the cup, took in the trees growing on the ledges above, and went from the girl to the two bearded men who had now scrambled down and stood beside her. "Last thing I remember, Sandy, we were back there in Akbad's cave. A wind was blowin.' It's still blowin', by golly! I can feel it! But—what happened, Sandy?"

"That's what I was just asking this lady," King answered.

"We'll talk about that later," the girl spoke. "Right now we've got to get out of here."

"Okay, partner, up you come," one of the men said, bending over King and helping him to his feet. He was the tired voice that King had heard. "Name's Greg," he said. "Greg Dawson. Let's get moving. When Leda says we've got to get out of here, she knows what she is talking about."

Dawson helped King to the base of the wall, started to help him up, but long before they got to the top it was King who was helping Dawson instead of the other way around. King realized why Dawson had sounded tired, why he had made no effort to descend the walls of the cup and help them. Dawson was as tired as his voice indicated. The man was completely worn out. He was panting heavily before they scaled the wall.

"Sorry, old man," he said. "Not much left in me."

"What's wrong?" King asked.

"Wrong? Oh, nothing much. It was just my turn to run yesterday. I'm kind of worn out today."

"Run?" King questioned. There was something in Dawson's tone of voice that horrified him.

"Yes. Oh. I forgot you didn't know about the running. Well, you'll learn soon enough."

BEFORE King could question him further the girl Leda was urging them to be moving. Leading away from the cup, was a barely defined path that resembled a game trail. She plunged into it. Around them and behind the walls of the forest closed up. King had seen jungle before, the thick, heavy growths of the tropical rain forests but he had never seen jungle like this. The trees were giants rising hundreds of feet into the air. Clinging to them, descending from them, were masses of vines. King was perturbed by three things. He did not recognize any of the trees. They were all new specimens to him. There were no animals, no birds of any kind, in this forest. The thick foliage of the trees overhead closed a roof over them. Down on the ground everything was cool and dark. Somewhere in the distance King heard, or fancied he heard, the droning of a vast pipe organ. Somehow the sound sent a chill through his body.

The girl led them at a rapid pace, too rapid for Dawson, who motioned for them to go on and dropped behind. King noticed that Leda was leading them over hard ground where it was possible and that she was apparently making every effort to hide their trail. She never moved a leaf on the ground, never broke a twig, never disturbed a piece of mould.

"They might find our trail," she explained, in answer to King's question.

"They?" he asked. "Who are you talking about?"

She did not answer but King noticed that she was constantly on the alert. Her eyes watched every tree, every open space, every break in the foliage above them. She moved with the lithe alertness of an Indian who suspects danger and to whom alertness is second nature.

"This way," she said, pointing to a stretch of solid rock at the base of an overhanging cliff. "Keep close to the cliff."

In single file, they followed. Somewhere around was the sound of falling water. She led them to it. A river flowing from the higher ground dropped fifteen or twenty feet in a waterfall. Below the pool was an eddy of green water that constantly circled back under the waterfall.

"Follow me," the girl said. She dived into the pool; cutting the surface of the water with hardly a ripple. King hesitated. Her head appeared. Treading water, she moved with the circling eddy toward the waterfall, motioning for him to follow. He dived into the pool. Splashes as he came to the surface told him that Carson and Sin Yul had followed. The eddy promptly carried them behind the fall. There Leda, her short dress of tanned skin glistening with drops of water as it clung to her, extended a hand to help them up on the ledge where she was waiting. A natural cave, dark and wet, led off into subterranean passages.

"We have survived because of this cave," she said. "They haven't found it yet."

AGAIN the allusion to the mysterious "They." Again she did not choose to explain. Instead, telling King to take her hand, and Sin Yul to take King's hand, and Carson to do the same and bring up the rear, she led them into the cave. King did not resist. Like blind lambs, they might be following her to the slaughter. King trusted her. She had blue eyes and freckles on her nose and she spoke English. But, for that matter, Akbad had spoken English.

The trail she followed led upward but the climbing was somehow easy, much easier than climbing out of the pit had been. Here the invisible wind was not buffeting them. King realized the wind had not blown outside the pit.

King lost all track of distance. They might have gone a mile, or five miles. In the darkness, he had no way of knowing. Leda entered a small natural room. Through an opening in the farther wall sunlight was streaming. The place was primitively furnished. Several wicker chairs, apparently handmade, a table chopped out of tree trunks, two beds covered with the skins of animals.

There was a man in the room. He rose when they entered.

"I want you to meet my father," Leda said.

The man was tall and thin. His clothing was in tatters, his cheeks were hollow, his face covered with a beard. Like Dawson, he looked like a person who was tired. Only his eyes were alive. He shook hands with them, inquired their names.

"I can't say that I'm glad to see you," he said. "For your sakes, I am sorry. But you are here and that is that. My name is Sorenson, James Sorenson, one time of the department of natural history of the Field Museum—"

"Sorenson!" King gasped. "Not Professor Sorenson!"

Sorenson bowed. "The same," he said. "You have heard of me?" He seemed pleased.

"Only that you disappeared, as we seem to have disappeared, somewhere in Burma several years ago."

Sorenson fixed him with keen eyes. "Yes," he said at last. "My daughter and I disappeared. And since you are here, of course you disappeared in the same manner."

"Well," King said. "Then at last we've come to the place where we can find out something."

Sorenson smiled, a little gravely. "Some things I can answer," he nodded. "But all things, no. No, there are things here in this cursed land and things about that infernal temple where Akbad rules that I do not even begin to understand. But what I know I will tell you." He shook his head, hesitating as if not knowing quite where to begin, then started his story.

CHAPTER FIVE

"THE first question I want to ask is," King said, "where are we?" It was the question he had been carefully keeping out of his mind ever since he had regained consciousness in the cup, in the pit in the granite. Where were they? A wind had pushed at them. It had blown them—where?

Sorenson nodded gravely. "I know," he said, sympathy in his voice. "I wish I could tell you where you are. It would help you. It would even help me."

"You mean, you don't know?"

"I'm afraid I don't," the scientist answered. He tugged at his beard, half shut his eyes in a fretful frown. "The name of this place I do know is Akkan. But whether Akkan is Earth a million years after we knew it, or Earth a million years before the human race appeared on it, or whether Akkan is one of the planets of our solar system, or whether it is a planet of a solar system ten thousand light years from Earth. I do not know."

"What?" King shouted. "What in thunder are you talking about?"

Like mad ghosts, Sorenson's words were dancing through his mind. The Earth as it was a million years in the past! The Earth as it might be a million years in the future! Maybe not even Earth! Maybe some other planet of the solar system, maybe a planet belonging to an entirely different system! Was Sorenson mad? Was this the drivel of a warped mind?

"That's right," Sorenson answered. His voice was firm and calm. "I don't know. I don't know whether even Akbad knows, whether those devils out there…" He gestured toward the round hole that served as a window. "…whether they know. You see, where we are all depends on where the Earth current took us."

"Earth current?" King questioned.

"You felt it in the pit," Leda spoke in explanation. "It felt like a wind. That wind is what Daddy calls the Earth current."

"Yes," Sorenson nodded. "That is the Earth current. Exactly what it is I don't know but I think it is a natural Earth current, a flow of some unknown force. It is like gravity except that gravity is a known Earth current that affects everyone everywhere. This current is unknown and, on Earth, it seems to exist only in the heart of one particular mountain in an unexplored region of Upper Burma."

KING nodded grimly. He was familiar with gravity and he could not well doubt that other, similar currents could exist. Whether Sorenson knew what he was talking about or not, King could not doubt that the Earth current actually existed. He had felt the pressure of that invisible wind. He remembered its buffetings too vividly to doubt its existence.

"But—" he said.

"We came through the heart of that same mountain." Sorenson nodded toward Leda. "We were Akbad's guests too, and so was Dawson, and everyone else who was ever here. The Earth current picked us up in that mountain and carried us here. The catch is—I don't know where it carried us."

He hesitated, groping for words. "Supposing you entered a cave and fell into an underground river. The water carried you away. You lost consciousness. Eventually you regained consciousness and found yourself in a strange land, miles away from your starting point. The Earth current is exactly like an underground river. It picks you up. It carries you away. Eventually it deposits you here. But where it has taken you, you don't know."

"You have to know," King insisted.

"No, you don't," Sorenson answered. "You don't know a damned thing about it and neither do I. The current may have carried you through time, it may have carried you through space, or it may have carried you through both time and space. You don't know what that current does to you after it has picked you up. So, when I say I don't know where we are, except that we are in the land of Akkan and that Akkan may be almost anywhere in the universe, I mean exactly what I say." He gestured toward the opening that served as a window. "Out there at night the sky is full of stars. I'm not an astronomer by any means but I've done a lot of exploration in my life. At times I've had to find my way by the stars, with the result that I know every major constellation on Earth. Night after night, ever since we came here, I've watched the stars in the sky of Akkan. If Akkan were on Earth, I would recognize some of the constellations. Of course, after the passing of a million years, the position of the stars would have changed so much as to be unrecognizable, which is why I say we may be on Earth in the far past or the far future. Because, watching those stars for a sign post to tell me where we are, I have not yet seen a constellation that I recognized."

THE hard words rammed home. Not only the words but the sincere manner in which they were spoken convinced King that Sorenson knew what he was talking about. The scientist was telling the truth.

The truth was—they were lost. Lost in the immensity of space of time, lost no telling where.

Akbad had hurled them here. Why?

What was the reason why that skinny monster had hurled them into the world of Akkan?

King looked at Sorenson.

The scientist was nodding. "I know what you're thinking," he said. "You want to know why Akbad tossed you into the Earth current. The reason is not hard to find. Akbad is a procurer for the imperial game preserves of Akkan. His duty in that cursed temple of his—and he fulfills it faithfully—is to procure game for the stocking of the royal preserves."

King's mind was racing. He noticed Carson. Carson had been carefully following the conversation. Carson looked scared now. Rare indeed had been the times when he had seen Carson show fear. Sin Yul's brawn face had turned almost pale. Dawson, who had entered alone, was sunk on one of the mats, a sickly grin on his face. Leda had moved to the window, was looking out, her face averted.

"Game?" King said huskily. "Game for the preserves? What are you talking about?"

"We are that game," Sorenson said grimly. "Just as, on Earth, a few millionaires owned game preserves where they raised game to hunt, so, on Akkan, there are royal preserves. The game the Akkans prefer to hunt, instead of deer or bear or lions or elephants, is human beings."

His grim voice slipped into silence. The great game! Mackintosh had talked about a game, had said the murderers on his heels had been playing a game. This was the game, a hunting game, the hunting of humans! It was not without historical precedents, of a sort. The Romans, in the days of the decadence of Rome, had put gladiators in the ring to hunt humans. The Akkans used humans as their prey in the game preserves.

King swallowed, braced his shoulders. "I think they will find we are rather tough game," he said.

"They've already made that discovery," Sorenson answered. "That's why they like humans in their preserves, because men are good fighters, because they fight back, because they're hard to catch and hard to bring down. Because men make excellent sport! These are the reasons why they like us. We give them a good snap before we go down. What is it, Leda?"

FROM the window, the girl was motioning for them to come near.

"Look..." she whispered.

127

Below the window was a long, sloping valley. Heavily forested, a stream wound down the center. A rocky glade was visible almost immediately below the opening.

King's eyes swept the valley, jerked abruptly to a halt. He had been looking down, searching for what Leda had seen. The thing she saw was not down there on the valley floor. It was hanging in the air not fifty feet from the opening.

A clear bubble of glass! It hung in the air like a huge raindrop glistening in the sunlight. It was slightly flattened at the bottom. On one side a door was visible and the interior revealed some simple machinery, apparently used to control the bubble. King's eyes were not on the bubble. His whole attention was concentrated on the occupant.

Standing erect in the bubble, controlling it while she keenly scrutinized the ground below, was a girl.

It was the girl whose picture had hung on the wall of Akbad's temple, the girl who had been painted by that master artist whose marvelous work had been on display.

A painting of her was in Akbad's temple. Here, in Akkan, she rode in a bubble of glass. King's heart leaped when he saw her. At this distance, there was no chance of his being mistaken. It was the same girl. She was so near he could see the graceful curve of her throat, the alert way she turned head as she scanned the ground below.

"Who—who is that?"

King heard Leda's sharp indrawn breath. Glancing at her, he saw that her face had gone completely white.

"That—that is Avena," she whispered. "She—she is the princess of Akkan."

"What is she doing there?"

"Watch!"

Out of the corner of his eyes, he caught a flicker of movement in the glade below. Down there a man had darted out of the growth of trees, had looked around, and then hastily had darted back. The movement was so fast that King was not certain he had seen it. But Avena had seen it. King saw her move the controls in the glass bubble. It slipped soundlessly through the air, hung over the glade, poised there. From an opening in one side of the glass bubble a tiny white sphere was released. King's first thought was that Avena had dropped a bomb. Then he recognized the sphere.

A BILLIARD ball! One of Akbad's floating billiard balls! The same kind of milky white sphere that had passed completely through Mackintosh!

"Lord!" he whispered.

"You know what the white ball is?" Leda asked.

"I know what it *does*," he answered. "I saw a man down there. Who was it?"

"Dillon," the girl answered. "You remember him. He was with Dawson at the pit when I came up."

"I remember him. Bird-voice. He ran all his words together. But what's he doing down there?"

"It is his turn," Leda answered, "to run today."

"His turn to run—"

"Watch…"

The glass sphere of Avena hung poised over the trees. Below it, the little white ball was darting in and out among the branches something like a bird dog covering an overgrown field in search of the scent of prey. Ahead, in the glade, was another flash of movement as Dillon showed himself for an instant. Instantly Avena sent her glass bubble toward him, the billiard ball whirling out of the trees and dashing ahead of her. King caught his breath.

"You are watching," Leda's slow voice said, "the hunting of Avena."

"So I gathered," King said. His voice was dry and raspy, like a dull file cutting soft metal. In his mind was turmoil. On Akbad's palace wall he had seen the painting of this girl; she had looked to him like everything that was beautiful and good. The instant he had seen the picture he had known that all his life he had been looking for her. Now he had found her, in the incredible land of Akkan, riding in a bubble of glass, a huntress of men. The thought was a knife turning in his heart. He watched the scene below.

Avena in her glass sphere hovered over the spot where Dillon had last been seen, the billiard ball ranging through the trees below her. Now it was visible, now it was hidden. Down there somewhere, King knew Dillon must be watching for it, his head turning nervously, watching, trying to hide. King knew what Bird-voice was thinking. Death was looking for Dillon and Dillon knew it. Suddenly the glass bubble moved again, farther away this time.

"He's showing himself too often," Leda said fiercely. "He's taking too many chances."

KING silently watched the hunt continue. Avena in her glass bubble hung poised over the forest, poised and watchful. A big game hunter on the slope of a hill, knowing there was a deer in a thicket down below him, would look like this, peering intently down, his gun ready, Avena moved silently, following her prey. Each time she moved, she went farther away. Suddenly the glass bubble stopped moving.

Dim and far off, but still frantic with fear, a scream trembled in the air. It swiftly died into silence. King watched. Avena sent her glass bubble down into the trees. For a minute she was out of sight. Then the sphere rose into the air again. Dangling on a hook below it was a human body. Swiftly it slid away into the distance. Avena was taking her game home. Another mounted head for her trophy room. King turned away. Leda, her head pillowed on her arm, was leaning against the wall. Her shoulders were shaking with sobs.

"One thing I would like to ask," King said. "You said it was his turn to run today? What did you mean?"

Leda turned. The tears were bright on her cheeks. "We take turns," she said.

"Go on."

She dabbed at her eyes. "This cave is the only place that is safe," she explained. "The Akkan don't know it exists. As long as they don't discover it, we are fairly safe. But when a hunting party comes near here, one of us goes out—to lure them away, so they won't find us."

Sorenson coughed. "There is another reason why we don't want them here," he hesitantly said.

King's eyes were on the girl. "So Dillon deliberately exposed himself?" he questioned.

She nodded.

King swallowed. Bird-voice, that little man, had been a hero. Remembering the way Dillon had looked, his ragged clothes, unshaven face, careless manner, it was hard to think of him as a hero. But you couldn't tell what was inside a man by the way he looked. Inside, Dillon had had everything that a man might need.

A sudden thought shot through King's mind, jerked his eyes back to the girl. *"We* take turns?" he snapped. "Does that mean that you—you—"

Fire flashed in her eyes. "Of course I take my turn. Everyone does, except Daddy, and we won't let him do it, because…because…" Her voice faltered, stopped.

King did not need to be told why Sorenson was not permitted to take a turn in the grim game of hide and seek played through the forest outside. The scientist wouldn't have a chance out there. He was too old for games, especially for games played here in the land of Akkan.

DAWSON was sitting on the floor. "It was my turn to run yesterday," he said slowly, "I was lucky. I got away. Mostly we do."

"Oh."

Dawson's fingers balled into fists, the knuckles showing white. Muscles knotted at the corners of his jaws. "Dillon was the best damned tail gunner who ever knocked a Zero out of the sky," he said slowly. "Sometime—sometime maybe I'll get a chance to get even for him. Sometime, damn them—" He choked, rose abruptly, stumbled from the room. King watched him go. Dawson, then, and Dillon had been American fliers forced down in Upper Burma. Some of those fliers had come here. King knew the feeling members of the same crew of fighting men had for each other and he knew how Dawson felt.

"Next time it's my turn," he said.

"And after that, it'll be my turn," Carson spoke.

Sin Yul gibbered some unintelligible words under his breath.

Sorenson plucked at King's sleeve.

"There is another reason why we do not wish the Akkans to discover this cave," he said. "Come. I will show you."

CHAPTER SIX

SORENSON felt his way through the darkness, pushed against what seemed to be solid stone. Slowly a section of stone moved away. Light streamed through an open door. The scientist motioned for King to follow.

The room that lay beyond the door was large. Soft glow lamps shed a sheen of blue light from the ceiling.

The room was full of machinery and men.

The men startled King. Although he hadn't had time to think about it, he had assumed that Sorenson and Leda, Dawson, Carson, Sin Yul, and himself were the only humans in Akkan. But there were men here, fifteen to twenty of them; all of them busy.

"Technicians," Sorenson explained, pride in his voice. "Some were radio operators, some navigators, some of them were pilots. It seems a war had started..." He sounded puzzled. "...and these men were flying bombers until they made forced landings in Upper Burma—"

"I know about that," King said.

"Oh. Well, Akbad gathered them up and sent them here and they brought with them some knowledge I had needed badly, but had lacked. You see, I am a scientist of sorts, but I know nothing about radio or high frequency electro-magnetic radiations, or things of that kind. These men do know these things, and..." Pride showed in his voice, and more than pride, hot anger, and a grimness too deep for words. "...with their help we have almost completed something that will surprise the hunting parties of Akkan when they enter the game preserves."

He pointed toward the far side of the room. A glass bubble similar to the one in which Avena had ridden was sitting there. Dismantled now, every part stripped from it. All over the room men were working with these parts, studying them, poring over them.

"That bubble fell out of control," Sorenson explained. "The Akkan who was riding in it broke his neck." He sounded happy about that. "The boys tell me they have solved the mystery of its operation. Hillson there…" He pointed to a stooped, black-haired man who was squatting down and staring at the stripped bubble through thick-lensed glasses. "…has been most helpful. He was an expert on electro-dynamics before he entered the army and I suspect was something of a fanatic on the subject. Isn't that right, Hillson?"

Spoken to, Hillson grinned. "Aw, Doc," he said. "What if I was a little nuts? You don't have to tell everybody about my weakness." He looked King over. "A new rookie, eh? Glad to have you with us. Do you know anything about electro-dynamics?"

"I'm afraid I don't," King admitted.

"Oh well…" Hillson had already lost interest in him and had turned back to the glass bubble. King grinned. He knew the type. The only thing that interested Hillson was that glass bubble and how it worked, especially *how* it worked. Hillson was the type that had kept the bombers flying, the fighters going up, in spite of hell and high water, the mechanical geniuses that America had produced in such large numbers, men who had seemed to need only a strip of tin, a length of wire, a couple of dry cells, and a pair of pliers to build anything.

ALL the men in the room seemed to be of this type. King had seen grease monkeys digging into a motor looking for a bug. They kept looking until they found it. He had seen colonels come down to watch a crew going over a plane, he had seen the colonels stand around and watch and itch for a while, then grab a wrench and dig in and damn the rank.

A sandy-haired youth—he didn't look like he was out of his teens—pulled at the scientist's sleeve.

"Dr. Sorenson?" he said timidly.

"Ralph? What is it, my boy?"

"I think I've got it, sir."

"You think you've got it?" Sorensen asked excitedly.

"I'm not sure, of course, but I *think*—"

Sorenson was following the youth across the room. He had forgotten all about King. Sorenson stared at something on the bench.

"Everybody come here," he called excitedly.

The men left their work and clustered around the scientist and the youth. Even Hillson reluctantly dragged himself away from his beloved glass bubble. A hushed air of excitement fell over the room. King followed the group.

"Show them, Ralph; show them what you have discovered," Sorenson urged.

King leaned forward, saw what lay on the bench. It was one of those damnable billiard balls, one of those horrible instruments of death that Akbad and Avena had used! He caught his breath.

The sandy-haired youth picked up the billiard ball. "I think," he said, "I think I've discovered how these things work."

"Show us…" Sorenson said.

The youth laid the ball back on the bench. He picked up what seemed to be a rather unusual finger ring set with a single large glittering jewel.

"We got these from the dead Akkan," he explained, slipping the ring on his finger.

"Watch, now."

He made no move, did not in any way attempt to manipulate the ring. A look of concentration appeared on his face deepened. He was holding up his hand for all to see the ring. Slowly, a tone at a time, the jewel was changing color. It had been white when he had picked it up. Now, as the look of concentration deepened on his face, the stone was becoming a soft violet color. Oblivious of everything else, he watched the ring, concentrating his gaze on the jewel. A minute ticked by, another.

"Watch out!" someone yelled.

THE billiard ball had risen from the bench and was floating in the air. King's instantaneous thought was that this damnable menace had somehow come to life and was loose in the room, threatening all of them with the terrible death that lay within it. His hand dived toward the gun that should have been holstered at his hip, came away empty. He crouched. He knew how deadly that ball was. The others knew it too. Their reaction was involuntary. Except for Sorenson and the youth, they ducked. Hillson reached for a wrench.

"There is no danger," the youth called out. "I'm making it move. Watch…"

His gaze still concentrated on the jewel in the ring, the lines of concentration deepened on his face. He did not look at the ball, but apparently at his command, it began to dart about the room, ducking, swerving, going through the agile dance that King so well remembered. All eyes were focused on it. Slowly, it came back to the bench, came to rest.

The youth sighed, wiped perspiration from his face, and removed the ring.

A babble of voices broke out.

"Ralph Rogers, how does that damned thing work?"

"Is it radio controlled, Ralph?"

The youth dabbed at the sudden perspiration on his forehead. "It is not radio controlled," he said. "It is more subtle than that. I am not quite certain but I am almost sure it is controlled by means of thought radiation. It is made of a peculiar type of crystal that has the property not only of defying gravity but of moving and changing its characteristics in accordance with the mental commands of the person in control of it. The real secret is in the ring and the ball is controlled through that. The ring was originally attuned to the personality of its Akkan owner. I managed to alter the tuning, to bring it to resonance with the radiations from my own mind. Later, I'll tell you how I did that. Now it is sufficient to tell you that you can see and hear and speak through the ball, you can send it anywhere you want it to go, and if you so desire, you can cause it to emit a type of radiation that will sear through almost anything that stands in its way—"

KING was no longer listening. Not being a mechanic, how the ball worked was not as important to him as it was to this group of wizard gadgeteers. The important thing to him was—they had a weapon with which to fight the Akkans.

"If we can get a supply of those balls—" he whispered. "Sorenson, where can we get some more of those things?"

The scientist turned to him. "The only source I know is the armory of the Akkar, in the city."

"Then that's where I'm going," King said.

Faces turned toward him. He was a newcomer in the group. They didn't know him, didn't know what he could or couldn't do. They were sizing him up. Hillson looked him over as if he were a special kind of glass bubble. Rogers, the sandy-haired youth, stared at him. Sorenson's shrewd gaze reappraised him.

"Shall we give this mission to Captain King?" the scientist questioned.

One by one through the group voices began to speak.

"He looks like the man for the job."

"I think, if anybody can do it, he can."

"Okay by me."

King grinned. "Thank you, gentlemen," he said. "When do I start?"

CHAPTER SEVEN

"THERE is Akka, city of Akkan," Sorenson said, pointing.

They were on the side of a hill, looking down. Below them, miles in extent, lay the city. Stone buildings lined broad streets bordered by gigantic trees. Parks were visible everywhere, with fountains shooting sprays high into the air. A few glass bubbles were visible, lazily ascending or descending, floating through the air carrying Akkar riders on errands. Vaguely audible was the sound of music, weird, unearthly, the soft, sighing strains of some tremendous pipe organ.

King looked at the city. Here a race had labored for generations—centuries past the counting—piling gray slabs of stone on top of other stones, building a city, developing a civilization, creating arts, investigating the sciences. The builders of Akkan had been artists, the graceful lines of the buildings, the way the parks were laid out, proved that. They had been scientists, the glass bubbles, the deadly floating balls, proved that. *Had been.* Automatically, without quite realizing why he did it, King put the accomplishments of the Akkar in the past. They had made steps toward greatness, building this city as a monument to their efforts. But something had happened. They had gone so far and then had stopped. Their city was falling away into ruins. The buildings, many of them, were falling down, the roofs falling in, needed repair work not done. Rubble from falling buildings had spewed into the streets. No effort had been made to clear it away.

"They made their bid for greatness," Sorenson was speaking. "You can see the evidence of it down there. But something happened to them and they fell short of their goal, stopped development, started backward. Yes, something happened…"

He sounded a little sad.

"What do you think happened to them?" King questioned.

"Possibly the land no longer produced food in sufficient abundance," Sorenson answered. "Maybe the climate changed. Possibly they ceased reproducing in sufficient numbers. A number of things may have happened. Sometimes races just seem to lose the will to live and start dying away. In this case, I think I know what happened. They persisted in clinging to a basic pattern that is sound

139

for a primitive tribe, but which spells doom to any race that tries to cling to it in more advanced stages of civilization."

"What pattern is that?" King asked.

"THE hunting pattern," the scientist answered. "Where hunting is necessary for life itself, hunting is justifiable. But the Akkar reached a level of existence where hunting was no longer necessary. For thousands, perhaps tens of thousands of years, they were forced to hunt to live. Then the time came when they no longer had to hunt, but— hunting was so much a part of them that they could not give it up. So they continued it, and it became a perversion with them. Instead of hunting game for food—hunting to live—they began to hunt for thrills. This was all right, as long as hunting was only a relaxation, but they began to seek more and more thrills, and the time finally came—I'll bet on it—when they were hunting their own kind, for fun. No race that hunts its own kind can continue to exist. So, the Akkar started down. Their development stopped, they began to retrogress, to go backward. If we ever discover their full history, I think we will learn that the glass airships they use were invented hundreds of years ago and no improvements have been made since they were invented, that all the rest of their science is falling into decay—"

Sorenson's voice droned on, expounding the rise and fall of races. The scientist knew his stuff, but King was only half listening. It did not matter much to him how the Akkar had developed. It was enough to know that they were here and were a deadly menace not only to him but to every other human whom Akbad had thrust into the Earth current. He remembered what Akbad had said. "You Yanks make excellent players of the great game. In the future, we hope that more of you will have the opportunity of playing."

Plans might be going forward to dump humans by the carload lot here in this damnable game preserve! They would not be hard to obtain. King did not know how powerful the glass airships were but he suspected that terrible powers were leashed within them. Fifty of those bubbles, appearing on Earth, might be a match for all the air fleets the Allies possessed, fleets already disbanded or in the process of being broken up. What would happen if the Akkar came out of Akkan and with Akbad to lead them, descended on New York, or Chicago, or San Francisco? King preferred not to think about that.

"How many Akkar do you think there are?" he asked Sorenson.

"Fifty thousand—a hundred thousand. Who knows?" the scientist answered. "I have stood here on this hillside and watched them swarming by the thousands down there in the city, during one of their festivals. I can't guess their numbers. Too many. That much is sure. For that reason, you must be very careful in attempting to find and enter their armory. If they catch you, get a hint that we are here, they will swarm over these hills by the thousands looking for us."

King nodded. He had seen how carefully the men in the cave laboratory had looked him over before they agreed to let him try to enter the city. Their lives were in his hands. If he failed, the Akkar would come looking for them. No doubt the Akkar would be pleased. New game to hunt!

"I don't intend to get caught," he said. "Ready, Ralph?"

ROGERS nodded. The sandy-haired youth was going with him, for several reasons, chief of them being that he knew how to operate the floating ball. If they could penetrate the storehouse where the balls were kept, Rogers would be invaluable in determining what to take and what to leave behind. In his pockets, he had a small kit of tools to make adjustments on the floating balls, if they managed to obtain any. Rogers grinned. "Let's hop off," he said.

"Cal," King said, turning to Carson.

"I think I ought to go along, Sandy," Carson said. "Damn it, you may get into a spot where I would come in handy."

"I think I ought to go too," Leda interrupted. "After all, I've been almost inside the city and I know the way."

King grinned. "Cal, your job is to wait just outside the city, and if we're not back by tomorrow night, to come looking for us."

"You do all the work while I sit out here and twiddle my thumbs," Carson grumbled. "Damn it, Sandy, I belong in this thing with you."

"No sale, Cal. Your job—to sit around and wait—is as tough as mine and I know it. As for you, Leda—*Look out!*"

Looking over Leda's shoulder, King saw one of the floating balls. In the air over the trees at the base of the cliff, he glimpsed—a floating glass bubble. It had come on silent wings, floating just over the tops of the trees, and was upon them before they had the slightest warning of its presence. Peering eagerly down from the bubble was— Avena.

The huntress of Akkan was hunting again.

For a split second the floating ball danced behind Leda. Before she had time to move, it darted straight toward her.

King flung her to one side, the darting ball passing over his shoulder. It passed so close to him he could hear it hiss.

"Into the trees, everybody!" he yelled.

Out of the corner of his eyes, he saw Sorenson, Carson, and Rogers leap down the hill. Leda, with lithe agility, scrambled to one side. King stood in the center of the opening. Over his head, the ball buzzed like an angry hornet. He did not move. He made no attempt to hide.

It was his turn to run!

Yesterday Dillon had done the running, Dawson the day before. Today was King's turn.

He watched the ball.

IF IT came toward him, he was ready to try to dodge, but he had to give the others time to escape. He could hear a threshing in the undergrowth as Sorenson and Rogers fought their way downhill. Leda had disappeared. He was all alone in the glade. Above him, the ball was darting in circles. In the glass bubble above the treetops, he could see Avena looking down. She seemed surprised. Perhaps the fact that he did not run had startled her into momentary inaction.

"Run!" Leda called, from somewhere out of sight.

Simultaneously the ball moved toward him.

He leaped headfirst into the shelter of the trees. Behind him something went *brr-br-brr-rrr* like a small but vicious P-51 going into a power dive. An excited voice was yelling. Avena, screaming with the thrill of the chase, the ball transmitting her voice.

"Tallyho!"

All that was needed was the sound of the hunter's horn, the bugling of the hounds, to make this a foxhunting scene. King, racing through the trees, knew how the fox felt when he heard the baying of the dogs on his trail. It wasn't a good feeling. Compounded of hot rage and icy fear, it seemed to send surges of ice water racing through his veins.

Brr-br-rrr-brrr.

The ball buzzed like a hornet. Over his shoulder, King caught a glimpse of it. Ducking and dancing, it was trying to find its way through a tangle of vines. For a second it was caught in the tangle. Only for a second. The ball turned milky white. The smoking vines fell away from it.

It had burned its way through the tangle.

King saw it come toward him.

He ducked around a tree, dived under the low boughs of an overhanging evergreen shrub, got down on his hands and knees, and crawled like a fool.

Somewhere overhead Avena screamed in disappointment. He lay still, panting, listening. He could not hear the ball. It was moving silently through the tangle seeking him. He moved cautiously forward.

The main part of his task had been accomplished. He had drawn Avena after him, had drawn her away from the others. They were safe by now. Leda, her father, Carson, Rogers, safe. Somehow a glow shot through him when he thought of Leda. She was safe. That was very important.

There remained the job of saving his own neck.

"Those who take the tiger by the tail cannot easily let go," he thought.

CRAWLING under the limbs that were too low to let him stand upright, he slid forward. Just ahead, a rocky ledge rose up, barring further passage in that direction. He moved along the base of the cliff, keeping out of sight. Once, through an opening, he caught a glimpse of Avena in her bubble. She was behind and to the right, looking in his direction. The ball he could not see.

An open space lay ahead of him. He surveyed the surroundings, made certain he was not seen, dashed across the opening.

Brr-brr-brr, right behind him, like a mad hornet.

Avena screamed in delight.

King sprinted. Avena had known where he was hidden. She had kept the ball hidden, had waited for him to show himself, had pretended not to know where he was. He had fallen for the trap.

Brrrr!

The ball was so close he could almost feel it. Ahead, ten yards away, the growth of trees began again. King ran at full height, looking back, casting quick glances over his shoulder. The ball darted at him. He flung himself flat. It ducked down toward him, hit the ground ahead of him, and bounced. He kicked at it, felt a jolt of searing pain, then leaped among the trees. The ball gyrated upward out of control.

Out of control!

His kick had damaged it!

Brrrrr!

It spun in a circle, dived down between the trees, following the path he had taken. It appeared to be under perfect control again.

King, ignoring the pain in his foot, ran. A halfback in a broken field, a halfback dodging tacklers, never displayed more agility than he did. Diving through shrubbery, ducking around trees, getting down and crawling, he ran as he had never run before. And—he lost the ball. Slipping forward, he kept completely out of sight.

Ahead, the cliff turned. He stared at it, frowning. Caught in a corner, he would either have to retrace his steps or go far to the right. He chose to go to the right, then stopped.

The glass bubble of Avena was over the trees to the right, blocking his escape. He would have to go back.

Behind him, in the direction from which he had come, he saw the ball. Moving in complete silence, it was hunting stealthily through the undergrowth for him.

He was trapped.

He considered his chances, made his choice. He crawled under a heavy growth of shrubbery to hide. As long as he lay still, Avena would have a hard time spotting him. Meanwhile night was not far off. If he could remain hidden until darkness—but a movement in his hiding place held his eyes. He gasped in startled disbelief.

It was Leda who had moved. She had fled in this direction too. All unknowingly, King had followed her, had lured Avena to her hiding place.

Both of them were trapped.

"WHERE did you come from?" King whispered.

"Shhhhh… Don't make a sound…"

He was silent. Quietly he adjusted the foliage to cover him, lay without moving. Overhead the bubble of Avena floated. Whether or not Avena knew that Leda was also trapped here in this elbow of the cliff, he did not know, but certainly the huntress knew that he was here. He could see her watching the ground below like a hawk waiting to pounce. Now and again he caught glimpses of the ball questing through the foliage. It no longer made the *brring* sound but moved in absolute silence. Using it, Avena could search every nook in the corner of the cliffs. She could pry into every hole, look under every leaf if she wanted to.

King watched the sun. In half an hour the quick darkness of Akkan would fall. Could they remain hidden a half-hour?

The ball passed directly over them.

He held his breath. It hesitated—then drifted on. He followed it with his eyes, watching it through breaks in the foliage. It was near the cliffs now, searching along the base of the bluffs. Suddenly it turned, started straight toward them.

He tensed.

It passed directly over them. Without hesitating, it went straight to the glass bubble. The ship rose above the trees, moved off toward the city of the Akkar.

Avena had called off her dog, had given up the hunt for this day, had gone home. King watched the bubble disappear in the sky, got slowly to his feet, wiped sweat from his face.

"That was a close call," he said.

Leda rose, stumbled, clung to him for support. He saw she was shaking, her face an ashy white.

"Are you hurt?"

"No. I'm—scared. That's all. Just scared."

"Poor kid," He patted her arm. No wonder she had been scared. Even better than he, she knew the meaning of the hunting of Avena.

"I'll take you back to the others," he said. "Then I'll go on into the city tonight."

MOVING slowly through the trees, they started to retrace their steps. A shadow moved swiftly along the ground. King looked up. Avena in her glass bubble was coming out of the sun toward them.

The huntress had tricked them. She had pretended to leave but instead of quitting the hunt, she had gone in a huge circle and had returned to the elbow in the cliffs, guessing that her prey would reveal itself when she seemed to leave.

She had guessed right. Her prey had revealed itself.

"Damn her!"

King shoved Leda down out of sight into the tangle. For a split second, he thought of trying to hide too. Then he decided on another course of action, for two reasons. One reason lay in the fact that he really didn't have time to hide. The other reason lay in his memory of the way Akbad, and Avena, had acted on different occasions. When he had surrendered to Akbad. Akbad had seemed to regret his action. Akbad had wanted him to run, had expected him to run. When he hadn't run, Akbad hadn't known quite what to do.

When Avena had caught them in the glade, and he had faced her for a moment, she had seemed surprised.

King stepped boldly into the open. Avena saw him. The sphere leaped almost straight up as she brought it to a halt. Out from it the white ball darted. Straighter than any arrow in flight, it dived straight toward King.

He did not move. Hands on hips, he watched it come, waiting its charge. The split second the ball took to reach him seemed to stretch into a century. In that second, he grew years older. Every nerve in his brain yelled at him to run, every muscle screamed for release of the terrible tension built up in it.

He stood rooted to the ground.

Brrrrr!

Six inches from his chest the ball buzzed angrily. It spun upward in a tight arc. Like a dog charging on a leash and suddenly pulled back, it was jerked away from it. It seemed to turn somersaults in the air over his head.

King ignored it. He watched the glass bubble. Avena, surprise on her lovely face, was leaning over and watching him.

"Well?" he said.

SILENCE, broken by the angry *brrring* of the ball.

"Well!" The hard toughness of tempered steel rang in his voice. He had no thought that Avena could understand him but perhaps she would grasp the meaning of the tone. The ball, he knew, would transmit the vibrations of his voice to her.

"What—what sort of creature are you?" Avena whispered, through the ball. The words, or the impulses entering his mind, were in English. He had no time to be concerned with the miracle that brought her words to him in an understandable tongue. He could talk to her and she to him. How that was done Rogers could explain later. If there was a later!

"Look in your trophy room!" he answered. "Your trophies should tell you what kind of a creature I am."

"I'm not talking about that."

"What are you talking about?"

"Well...you came out into the open."

"Are you surprised to have your game talk to you, to have it face you rather than run from you?"

"All the others ran." There was something here that she couldn't understand. The others had run. He hadn't run. This puzzled her.

King heard the puzzled note in her voice. He dared to breathe.

"Didn't it occur to you that sooner or later you would meet someone who wouldn't run?"

"No. I thought—"

"You thought that humans were created to run for you." Hot anger boiled in his voice. "When one of them doesn't run, you're so damned surprised you don't know what to do with yourself!"

"This—this is no way to speak to the Princess of Akkan!" She was angry, too—mad clean through.

"As to that, I wouldn't know," King said. "I never met a princess before, so naturally I don't know how to talk to one. But from what I've seen of the princess I have met, it's all right with me if I never meet another one."

"You—you dare—"

The ball *brrred.*

"I dare anything. I've been in battle, lady. In battle men get so mad and so tired that they don't give a damn what happens. I'm mad now, and tired too, if you want the whole truth, and I don't give two hoots in Georgia what happens next."

What he said was part truth. He was angry and tired and largely he didn't give a damn. But his actions resulted from more than anger. There was cold calculation in them. The Akkar prized bravery. If they prized it enough, he might, just possibly might, remain alive. He had no choice. If he played his cards right, Avena might do anything. If he played them just a little wrong, if he made her too angry, she might—well, there was the ball circling over his head.

"Do your damnedest, Princess of Akkan."

"Oh! You fool! You hopeless fool!"

"Am I?"

"Have you no fear of death?"

"Lady, by rights I should have been dead long ago. I'm living on borrowed time. So, if you knock me over, it won't make any difference."

AVENA had brought the bubble lower. He could see her clearly now, the anger in her face, in the hot sparkle of her eyes. She was the most beautiful woman he had ever seen.

"Why do you stare at me like that?" she demanded.

He told her. "All my life I've carried a dream of you in my heart," he answered. "Now, I've seen you."

"A dream of me? But that's not possible. You never saw me before."

"So I never saw you before? So what? I've dreamed of you just the same."

"And now that you have met me?"

King was silent. His face showed his thoughts.

"So I am not as beautiful as you had dreamed?"

"If anything, you are more beautiful. It's—it's just that I hate a coward—"

"A coward? Surely you do not think of me as a coward?"

King took a deep breath, and plunged. "How else can I think of you? From the safety of an airship the like of which I've never seen before you come hunting creatures that have no way to defend themselves. You stay up there where you're safe and sound, and you send that thing—" He gestured up toward the whirling ball. "to hunt us down. You don't take any risks of any kind whatever. If that isn't cowardice, I don't know cowardice when I see it."

"Oh!" She was angrier now than ever, so angry that for a second he thought she was going to launch the ball at him. "The Akkar have always hunted this way. It is considered a very brave thing to come here into the forests and hunt the wild beasts that Akbad sends here. The Akkar are the bravest of all people—"

"Who says so?"

"Who says so? Why—Why—"

"The Akkar!" King said bitingly. "Who else would say so but the Akkar? If you want the opinion of anyone else, ask the trophies in your game room what they think. Ask *me...*"

SURPRISE showed again on her lovely face. And perplexed thought.

Living in Akkan, an Akkar, she had never thought that another race might have a different opinion of the bravery of the Akkar. She had never met a member of another race. Killed them, yes, but talk to them, no. Now she was talking to one and she was finding it perturbing.

"But we are brave."

"Prove it!"

"Prove it? How?"

"Go back to your city and find the biggest strongest, bravest Akkar of your race. Bring him back here and drop him down on the ground and let him face me unarmed. Then we shall see who is brave. Meet me with no weapons. Bring your champion, your greatest hunter—"

"That would be Lardon. But he wouldn't come. And if he did come—"

"He would sit up there in an airship and send a ball down after me," King grated. "He would be afraid to meet me face to face."

He had her going! She didn't know what to say. Her anger was gone. It had been replaced by perplexity. And, most important of all, she was no longer thinking of him in terms of another trophy to ornament her game room.

"Lardon wouldn't come," she repeated.

"Of course he wouldn't come. I knew he wouldn't. I've never seen him, but he is an Akkar, and all Akkar are cowards."

"All?"

"Every last damned one of you!"

"Is that so?"

"Yes."

"We'll see about that..." As she spoke, she was working the controls of the airship. King's thought was that she was going to leave. He expected to see the bubble rise above the trees, head back toward Akka. It didn't rise. It dropped swiftly to the ground, crunched through the shrubbery, came to a halt. Opening the door, Avena leaped out, came toward King.

"You said no Akkar would dare to meet you face to face, unarmed. Well, I'm meeting you. Now let's see what you are going to do."

"Well, I'll be forever damned!" King gasped. "No, don't do that!" Her hard little fists were beating at him. He pushed them away.

"I'll show you!" she panted. "You said we were cowards. I'll show you. Release my hands!" She was furiously angry. King held her easily and pretended not to notice the ball *brring* overhead. She was not wearing a finger ring to control the ball but he suspected the single gleaming jewel on the chain around her neck served the same purpose. Did he dare grab the chain...snap it? Without the ball, she would really be helpless.

"Turn me loose!" she demanded.

KING released her. She drew herself up to full height. "All right, brave man. I'm here. Why don't you do something?"

King shrugged, glanced up at the ball. "With that thing up there, you ask me to do something!"

"It won't harm you."

King laughed.

"So you are afraid of it, are you? All right, I'll send it away."

Silently obeying her unspoken command, the ball slid through the open door in the glass bubble, came to rest on the floor.

"Now, it's gone. I'm powerless to defend myself."

"Scarcely that, Avena."

She spread her hands, to show they were empty. "But I have no weapon. See for yourself. I am meeting you on equal terms."

Was she trying to kid him? The ball might be in the glass bubble but at her mental command, it would leap into action in something less than seconds. He shook his head.

"Coward!" she challenged.

"Even if you were weaponless, I wouldn't fight you," he answered.

"Why not?"

"You're a woman."

"What difference does that make?"

"What difference! In your world is it a custom for men to fight women?"

"Certainly. Isn't it the same in the world you came from?"

"I should say it isn't," King answered. "Men do not fight against women. It wouldn't be a fair fight. No,

Avena, I won't fight you, not even if you removed the necklace from around your throat and threw it away."

"What?"

"Why this nonsensical farce?" King demanded. "You're pretending to be unarmed. What kind of a fool do you think I am? If you're so determined to meet me on equal terms, why don't you take that necklace off and throw it away?"

"How do you know about this necklace?"

"How— Why—" King suddenly shut up. He could have torn his tongue out. He had said too much! There was no way he could have known the ball was controlled through the necklace.

"For that matter, how do you happen to know my name? Twice, you have called me Avena. How did you learn my name?"

HER voice was challenging, suspicion filled, and shot through with sudden overtones of fear.

"I—you told me your name," King lied hastily.

"I did not. And I certainly did not tell you anything about the necklace. Where did you learn these things?"

Too late, King realized he had made a fatal error. As long as she thought of him as something a little more intelligent than a beast, he had a chance. Now she knew he knew too much, he knew more than he had any right to know. Her eyes narrowed to slits, were fixed on him.

Brrrr! Out from its resting place in the bubble the ball shot. It whirled overhead.

Ice-cold water flowed through King's veins. He had blundered, and she had caught him.

"Well?" she challenged.

He shrugged, spread his hands. "Wouldn't you like to know," he answered.

"Tell me, or—" She pointed upward toward the ball.

"Go to hell…"

Probably she did not know what hell meant but the tone must have revealed his meaning. Her face flushed. For a second, he thought she was going to launch the ball at him.

Instead she pointed toward the glass airship. "In there!" she ordered.

"In there?"

"Yes. Instantly."

She sounded like a tough top sergeant. Silently King obeyed.

The glass bubble lifted over the forest, moved swiftly toward the city of Akka. Avena, busy at the controls, said nothing. In equal silence King watched their approach to the city.

"Well, I started to this town," he thought. "But I certainly didn't expect to arrive this way."

Somewhere down in that city slipping away into ruin was an armory that he had to find, if he remained alive long enough. If he could manage to stay alive, he would have an excellent chance of finding the armory. And Carson, Rogers, probably Leda, would come looking for him. Leda would tell them what had happened. Carson would be sure to come.

"Why are you looking so grim?" Avena suddenly questioned.

"Was I?" King grunted. Then he grinned. "Sorry, I guess I'm not my usual cheerful self today."

Somberly she studied him. Then she smiled. "You're a strange person," she said. "But I like you."

"I was afraid of that," King answered.

CHAPTER EIGHT

ENTERING the city, the first place they stopped was the armory King was seeking!

Avena sent the glass bubble down in a long slant, down and into a long building that looked like, and was, a hangar. Made of stone, slate-roofed, it was badly in need of repair. Inside were great numbers of the strange airships. Some were obviously hangar queens, being stripped for their parts, others were being repaired, still others were ready for use. The hangar was filled with workmen, most of them old, all of them slow moving. Lackadaisically, one came forward when Avena grounded her ship. Ducking his head in what was apparently intended to be a gesture of obeisance, he stood aside while they got out of the ship. Then he entered it, moved it off to a line of others, and began to inspect it.

"Come with me," Avena said.

The billiard ball had followed her out of the ship. As they walked toward a door in the far corner of the vast hangar, it floated over their heads. King noticed that it seemed to move sluggishly. Avena rapped on the door. It was opened for her and they entered. King took one look around. His eyes narrowed.

This was the armory! There was no question about it. They had entered a long, low-ceilinged room. Down both sides were workbenches, dozens of them—hundreds. Running behind the benches was a series of cables with power-takeoffs coming down to each bench. Somehow or other it reminded him of a large storage-battery charging

THE HUNTRESS OF AKKAN

station, except that the equipment on the benches had never been designed to put power into any storage battery he had ever heard of. Besides, the benches did not hold batteries. They held the glowing balls, the deadly billiard balls of the Akkan. Each ball rested in a specially designed niche. Complicated machinery seemed to feed current to them.

The armory seemed to be short of manpower. Not over twenty-five or thirty of the benches had attendants. The benches at the far end of the long room seemed not to have been used for years.

An attendant, apparently the person in charge, came hobbling up to them. He was old and stooped. Button-black eyes peered out at them from wrinkled cheeks the color of shoe leather. He ducked his head to Avena.

"The *chad* needs recharging," she said. "Give me a fresh one."

"Yes, Princess. The Princess..." The shoe-button eyes darted toward King. "...the Princess is going to play a game?"

"That is none of your affair, Kathor!" Avena snapped. "Here; take this. And in the future, mind your own business." As she spoke, she was removing the necklace and its pendent jewel from around her neck. King realized that her voice was growing weaker and weaker. Kathor took the jewel then bobbed off, the ball floating behind him. Apparently at his direction, the ball slid into a niche on the nearest bench. He laid the necklace down, picked up another, then came bobbing back to Avena. She slipped the necklace around her neck. Up from the bench a ball darted. Dancing and darting, it gyrated in circles and took up a position directly above King's head.

THE HUNTRESS OF AKKAN

KING watched the whole performance with appraising eyes. "Hmmm," he said. "*Chad*, I gather, is your name for that thing." He nodded toward the ball.

"Yes," Avena answered. Her voice was strong and firm in his mind now, with no trace of weakness in it. "The *chad* are dependent upon stored energy. When all their current is used, we bring them here for recharging."

"Interesting. Very interesting. Who invented the *chad* and how does it work?"

"It was invented long ago," Avena answered. "As to how it works, I don't know." She shrugged. How the *chad* worked was of no interest to her. She didn't even know the name of the Akkar who had invented it. "Come with me," she said.

King followed her. "Sorenson was right," he thought. "The Akkar at one time made tremendous scientific advances. Then they stopped advancing. Now they're going back. She doesn't even know who invented that thing, and doesn't care."

In America every schoolboy knew the names of the men who built the first airplane, who designed the telephone, who invented the radio. In America these things were important. In Akkan, nobody cared. Or nobody except a group of trapped and desperate Yanks, hidden in a cave inside a mountain. They cared how the *chad* worked. They cared plenty.

Avena led King through the city. What had been dimly visible from the height overlooking Akka—the disintegration, the slow crumbling into ruin—was readily apparent here. The streets had not been cleaned for years. They were littered with smelly debris. A few Akkar were visible, picking their way along. Unlike Avena they were not protected by the *chad*. The sun, low on the horizon, was throwing long shadows across the town. The Akkar seemed to be hurrying to get out of sight before darkness fell but the ones they met stopped long enough to stare at King in undisguised amazement.

"I seem to astonish your fellow citizens," he observed.

"They are not citizens," she answered. "They are workers, free slaves. Only hunters can be citizens."

"Ah. Hunting, I take it, is the most important activity of your race."

"Of course." Surprise was in her voice. "What else could be important?"

"Well, I could think of some things," King muttered. "Like cleaning up these streets and repairing the buildings, but no matter. It's your world; run it as you please."

She looked startled. "Are you daring to criticize the Akkar?"

"Nothing like that," King answered. "Merely a suggestion." He didn't want to set off her hair-trigger temper again, or not until he had discovered where she was taking him.

HE soon got the answer to that question. Avena led him into what had once been a palace. Constructed along the same lines as Akbad's temple in Burma, it was composed of scores of buildings, all roughly grouped together to form a single structure. Avena entered the central hall. Here forty or fifty Akkar were seated around a long banquet table. Unlike the Akkar they had seen on the streets, each one around the table had a *chad* floating over him. When Avena entered the room, they greeted her with shouts of joy.

"Ho, Avena, back from the hunt?"

"What luck, Princess?"

"Did you get another head for your trophy room?"

Then they saw King. There was instant silence. The deadly billiard balls floating in the air seemed to tense themselves. They had been floating easily, like tiny captive balloons on a windless day. Now, as soon as King entered the chamber, they began their terrible dance.

The silence was broken by a voice. "What is *that?*"

"Where did it come from?" a second voice asked.

"What's it doing here?"

Avena, without answering, had seated herself at the head of the table. She clapped her hands. Slaves came running, bearing water, food, wine, which they sat before her. Ravenously she began to eat. King swallowed. Hunger was a gnawing knot in his stomach. Thirst had dried his throat. It seemed to him that he would give his life for a glass of that cool, sparkling water that Avena was drinking. The Akkar stared at him in a dumfounded amazement that he ignored.

"It's a man..." one of them whispered in awe-struck tones.

"It's human!" another said.

There was disgust in the voices, and unconcealed hostility. Avena ate on.

"Why does Avena bring that in here?" The questioner was a bullnecked, beefy individual seated at Avena's right.

"Am I answerable to you, Lardon?" Avena asked.

"No. Of course not. But—"

"But what?"

"Nothing," Lardon answered. His face reddened, veins pulsing in his forehead. He glared venomously at King as if the latter had caused his trouble with Avena.

"I chose to bring him here," Avena stated.

"But he's dirty," one of them protested.

"And he smells bad," a second added.

KING cleared his throat. Enough was enough. "I grant you I probably smell bad," he said. "I'm dirty and I'm also hungry and thirsty. But so far as the dirt and the smell goes, I don't see anybody in this joint who wouldn't be improved by a good GI scrubbing."

He wasn't sure they would understand him. He was sure enough of the operation of the *chad* to know whether his meaning would reach them. If they did understand him; and didn't like what he said, they could darned well lump it.

They understood him all right. Their faces showed it. Lardon started to get to his feet. "Of all the insolence—" he began.

"Sit down," Avena said.

Grumbling Lardon slid back into his chair. Avena pointed her thumb toward King, spoke between bites. "*He* said Akkar smells bad. He said all of us ought to work on the streets until we got them cleaned up."

Amazed incredulous silence held the group. To them, King belonged to an inferior species, to a type of animal that was good enough for purposes of the hunt but which could not be mentioned on the same breath with an Akkar. And this ragged, dirty, jungle beast was daring to criticize them! A growl ran around the group. Avena continued eating.

"He also said," she spoke again, "that the Akkar are cowards."

This really produced a buzz.

"Damn his eyes!"

"I'll have his heart's blood for this."

"He'll adorn my trophy room before another sun has set."

"Let me have him."

"No. Let me!"

A dozen of the *chad* were diving toward King at the same instant.

"Stop it!" Avena's voice rang out.

The balls were so close King could feel the heat from them as they were pulled away.

Questioning eyes turned toward the girl.

"He said the Akkar were cowards because we refused to meet him empty handed. He said killing him with the *chad* is no proof of our bravery. He said the only way we could prove our bravery to him would be to meet him on equal terms, either by giving him a *chad*, or a knife, or giving him any weapon we chose just so we had the same weapon. Was that what you said...man?" She was speaking to King directly now.

FOR a split second King hesitated, wishing he had that white throat between his fingers. Damn her! She had certainly turned the tables on him. But the deed was done and there was nothing to do except go through with it.

"That's what I said," he answered. "The Akkar boast of their bravery, citing their hunting exploits as proof. The Akkar think, because they go out and hunt us down, that they are proving themselves to be the bravest of all people. Instead they are proving themselves to be the biggest of cowards. If you want to show how brave you are, meet me on equal terms."

Open-mouthed, the diners stared at him. His words had certainly given them a new slant on themselves, a slant they speedily discovered they did not like.

Lardon, his face red with rage, turned to Avena. "Princess, let me destroy this—this—"

"Certainly, Lardon," Avena cooed. "I also think his insolence is unbearable. Destroy him."

Lardon leaped to his feet. The glitter in his eyes was almost maniacal. Over him, his *chad* darted toward King.

The Yank took one step forward. His left fist lashed out. It connected solidly with Lardon's jaw just in front of the ear. The Akkar turned a half-flip backward, hit the floor, and clawed like a cat as he tried to get to his feet. Momentarily he lost control of the deadly ball darting toward King. It lost momentum, drifted aimlessly. King turned to Avena.

"Enough of this," he said abruptly. "Kill me and have it done with. I've had enough of this torture."

She was staring at him in openmouthed admiration. "I didn't mean—" she started to say, then abruptly broke off. "Lardon! Stop it this instant. If you strike him from behind with the *chad* I'll have your head off your shoulders within an hour. Stop it."

King turned just in time to see the deadly ball pull away from him.

"But you said to destroy him," Lardon argued.

"I meant to meet him on equal terms and destroy him, *if you could!*" the girl answered.

"Meet him on equal terms—"

The princess nodded.

"But that is an impossibility. I am a hunter of Akkan. I would not dirty my hands with such trash as this."

"No?"

"No!"

"Then I think he is right, that you, at least, of the Akkar, are a coward."

IN that moment King knew, through no fault of his own, he had made a deadly enemy. Rather Avena had made an enemy for him. If he never did anything else, Lardon would kill him now. Probably the Akkar would not meet him in a fair fight—the mottled color on his cheeks showed he was afraid of that—but he would certainly make every effort to kill the intruder. King was suddenly angry, at Avena, for forcing such an issue. Why was she torturing him? If she wanted him killed, why didn't she order it done, and get it over with? She was speaking again, to him now.

"I believe you said you were hungry. Forgive me for neglecting you. It is our law that all guests shall be fed. Here...*catch!*"

From the plate in front of her she selected a morsel of meat, flung it at him. If he had been a hungry dog, she would have used the same gesture. There was contempt in the act and in her eyes was mockery.

The anger burning in King boiled over. He caught the meat, with all his strength flung it back into her face.

For a split second there was dreadful silence in the room. The hottest rage he had ever seen burned in her eyes. Then the rage faded. Wonder replaced it. And something of awe. For a moment her eyes were the eyes of a little girl, of a miss eight years of age, of a little girl looking adoringly at someone she loved more than anything else in the world. The wonder remained in her eyes. Silence held the room. With one hand she wiped her face clean.

"You know," she said slowly, "I am rather proud of you. When I found you out there in the forest I thought

THE HUNTRESS OF AKKAN

you were a bag of wind, a boaster, a braggart. Now I know I was wrong, that I misjudged you."

The wonder remained in her eyes.

"Yes, I am proud of you. And I think you were right about the Akkar, although I had never thought of them as being cowards. I also think you have something the Akkar need, and need badly."

"What do mean?" King whispered. He did not dare to trust himself to raise his voice above a whisper.

She smiled. The lights deepened in her eyes. "That will come later."

She clapped her hands. To the frightened slaves who came running, she said. "Conduct this man to the best chamber in the palace. Bathe him, provide clothing for him. Set the best food, the best wine, before him. Anything he wants he is to have, but he is not to leave the palace. Move!"

Slaves tugging at his arms, King found himself led across the room. Silence held the banquet table. Glittering eyes watched him go. Some of the Akkar were looking speculatively at Avena. The others, and Lardon was foremost among them, were glaring at him. His mind in turmoil, King allowed himself to be led away.

LATE that night Avena came to his rooms. Except for Kathor, the aged workman from the laboratory where the *chad* were charged, she was alone. They entered his room furtively, and King, seeing them, wondered at her choice of a companion.

"What do you want?" King questioned.

"We came to talk," Avena answered. Soft lights illumined the room dimly. King was struck by the change in the girl's manner. Before, she had been haughty, imperious, a queen by divine right, a huntress by centuries of tradition, a ruler, mistress of herself and of her people, one who knew her word was law. Somehow she had changed. The haughtiness had gone. She was almost humble now.

"First, let me admit I tested you," she said.

"Tested me?" King echoed.

"Yes. When I brought you into the presence of my nobles, I deliberately forced you into a dangerous situation, where you would have to prove yourself. Frankly, if you had shown yourself unworthy, if you had turned coward, if you had not lived up to your words, well, Lardon could have worked his will with you." For an instant, ringing steel was in the tones of her voice, revealing depths of character King had not suspected. Huntress she was, cruel and wanton killer, but weakling never.

"Even the way I tossed the food at you was part of the testing," she continued. Wonder and something of awe came into her eyes again. "Yes, I was proud of the way you met the test."

"Thank you," King said. Strong emotions pulsed through him. He sternly suppressed them. Better wait, better see, better find out what she wants. "You said something about some questions?"

"Yes. I—we—want to know—" she hesitated. A silent, inscrutable witness, Kathor, the ancient technician, stood and watched.

"About what?" King invited.

"About—the land beyond…"

"What?"

"The world beyond."

King stared at her.

"The princess means the world from which you came," Kathor interposed. The old man's voice was deep with bass bell tones. "We want to know about that."

"Oh…"

"We want to know about its customs, how the people live, what they eat and do they always have enough to eat, how they are governed and what kind of kings they have, and—" Avena ran out of breath.

"We want to know about your sciences," Kathor continued. "We want to know the location of your world, the natural laws that govern there. We want to know about your physics, the chemistry of your world, about the—" But King's mind refused the term. Kathor was referring to something that existed or was known in Akkan but which either did not exist or was not known on Earth.

"WHEW!" King whistled. "You certainly do want to know something," He studied Kathor, seeking the motive that lay back of the question. The old technician met his gaze squarely. King looked at Avena. She was eagerly watching him.

"Will you tell us?" she questioned.

"Why do you want to know?" he asked.

"That is none—" For a second her old imperious manner returned and she was again a ruler putting a subject into his place. Instantly she caught herself. Her tone changed. "We want to know and we have reasons for wanting to know. Isn't that enough?"

King grinned. "I guess it is," he answered. His reservations he kept to himself. Some things he would tell them. There was much he would keep to himself, until he knew the reasons they had for seeking the information. He began to talk.

He told them about Earth, the green planet that to him was lost in some vast immensity across or beyond a gulf that he did not begin to understand. Earth of the blue skies and the gray-green seas, of clouds and rain and sunsets and rainbows, of mountains and deserts, of polar ice caps and steaming tropical jungles. He had seen them all and he talked well. Kathor listened with almost torrid interest, a youthful light suddenly alive in his old eyes. "I didn't know...I couldn't guess... Imagine!" was all he could say.

"But the people," Avena interrupted. "I want to know about the people. Talk about them."

King talked about men, about Arabs and Chinese, Germans and Japanese, the English and the Norse, and the amazing Russians who groped toward something without knowing exactly what it was except that it was somehow colossal. He talked about the French and the Spanish and the Italians and the Negroes, about all the peoples on Earth, except one. Avena listened avidly now, Kathor with slightly less concentration.

"Tell us about your own people," Avena ordered.

King sighed. "I am an American," he said and he wondered what that meant. For America had taken all the races of Earth, all of them, had blended them together, and out of that blending had come no one knew exactly what, except that it, too, was somehow colossal. King tried to tell them about this.

"Who is your king?" Avena questioned.

"We have no king," he answered, surprised.

"No king?" Now Avena was surprised. So he had to explain that. When he had finished she seemed to understand, but he doubted if she really did understand. No one who was not an American ever really understood.

You had to be born in a land, to live in, to sweat, suffer, and work in it, before you really understood. Avena listened. And Kathor began to ask questions.

Kathor wanted to know about science. King answered, but now he dealt in half-truths, in evasions, in answers that were not clear. Kathor was not satisfied. Again and again he insisted that King explain more clearly. He did not get what he wanted. To explain too much was not wise, until King knew why the information was wanted. He did not know that. Nor were they willing to tell him.

Suddenly the light in the windows revealed he had talked all night. Kathor and Avena left as furtively as they had entered.

"But we will return," Avena assured him. "We want to know more." What was going on in that sleek head, King wondered?

THE next night they came again. And talked. The next night it was the same. Never did they reveal the purpose moving in the back of their minds. Each night they came and asked questions. Each day King discovered he was a prisoner. Everything he wanted he received; food, the best of care. But the door of the room was always locked and always the obsequious slaves who served him kept wary watch over him.

Then, just before noon, Kathor came for him. And he discovered what had been in their minds all the time. There was a glittering light in the eyes of the old technician when he entered the room.

"It's a great day for Akkan," he said. "Come. There are things for you to see."

Wondering, King followed him. Kathor led the American to what had once been a vast, open-air amphitheater capable of seating forty to fifty thousand people. It, like everything else in Akkan, was half in ruins but the central stage was still usable and the stone seats in the great half-bowl were still in place. There was something missing, however, and King saw at a glance what it was: the throng that once had filled this bowl, the horde that it had been built to accommodate. The people—they were missing. A scattering of Akkar were present, enough to fill the lower tiers, thousands where once there had been tens of thousands.

In the center of the stage, in a massive throne chair with a canopy over it to protect her from the rays of the sun, Avena was seated.

Below her, in a semicircle between her and the crowd, were her nobles, the hunting caste of Akkan, each with a *chad* floating over his head. The people in the stand had no *chad*. Only Avena and her hunters wore the deadly little floating balls.

"What is going on?" King questioned.

"This is the beginning of the Festival of the Laws," Kathor answered. "On this day the ruler of Akkan, now the Princess Avena, appears before her people, and announces the laws for the coming year."

"Ummm, you mean Avena makes all the laws of this country?"

"Naturally. I understand you do it differently in your country but we have done it this way in Akkan for centuries past the counting."

"Do the people obey her?"

"Certainly. Her word is law."

"Well I'm damned..." King said.

UNOBTRUSIVELY Kathor took him down among the crowd, sat down with him. King suddenly noticed that the aged technician was trembling. "What's wrong?" he asked.

"Shhhh! Wait. Watch."

The festival commenced. It started with all the trumpery and display of a barbaric people, with the fanfare of trumpets, the weird wailing of musical instruments unknown to the American. A procession of pages brought in a gold mace that was apparently the symbol of the power of the ruler. Avena accepted it. The trumpets blew again. Avena rose from her chair, extended the mace.

"The law controlling the rights of the people to life is extended for another year." Her clear voice carried over the whole assembly. The trumpets blew again.

"The law governing the rate of taxation is extended for another year, the rate remaining the same." Again her clear voice rang out. Again the trumpets blew.

Marveling at the customs of this strange people, King listened. The laws meant little to him but they seemed to mean a great deal to the assembled Akkar. They were listening attentively. Several times King saw some of them glancing around as though they were looking for someone. Every time their gaze seemed to seek out Kathor. The aged technician appeared not to notice. King sensed a tension growing in the crowd. Most of them were waiting to hear the voicing of the laws but some of them were waiting for—something else. For a period that seemed to be hours in length Avena announced the laws of Akkan. King could not see why this was important. These laws had been in force for centuries. She was merely continuing them in force. What was there to get excited about?

Some of the Akkar *were* getting excited.

Avena suddenly stopped speaking. Her gaze went over the assemblage as if she was trying to locate someone. Her eyes centered on King. She looked straight at him, as if she sought courage to continue. Then she smiled. Her firm voice rang out again.

"I have now come to the place where it is customary in the voicing of the laws to announce the law of the hunting of the nobles of Akkar."

A STIR ran through the assembly. This was not in the ritual. This was not in the script.

"I am ready to announce that law. *From this day forth the nobles of Akkan will cease from hunting, they will give up the beastly and degrading amusement that has done so much to bring this land and these, my people, to their present low state of civilization. My nobles will cease from hunting. There will be no hunting in Akkan, no hunting of any kind. My nobles, instead of hunting, will supervise the cleaning and restoring of this city to its former glorious condition. They will encourage the lagging industries, they will aid and abet the faltering sciences, and they will do everything in their power to make certain that Akkan and the Akkar resume their interrupted march onward and upward to the future.*"

Hot silence filled the huge bowl.

"I have spoken," Avena ended. She returned to her throne, sat looking out over the throng, waiting tensely.

Her word was law. She had ordered the end of the hunting in Akkan. In effect, she had destroyed the most cherished privilege of the upper classes. She had decreed what was nothing less than a revolution.

King's heart leaped up into his mouth as he listened to her words. *This,* this was what she and Kathor had been planning. This was what they had had in mind when they had questioned him. Revolution! They had wanted to know about Earth and the customs of its peoples so they could bring about reform in Akkan.

The hot silence was broken by a sound. King, on his feet, madly cheering.

"Atta girl, Avena! That's the best damned law that ever was passed in the whole history of this country!"

Heads turned in his direction. Kathor abruptly jerked him back to his seat.

"Shut up and wait!" the old technician hissed.

"Wait for what?"

"There is…ah…"

Down in the semicircle surrounding the raised stage on which Avena's throne was placed a noble was getting slowly to his feet.

"I cry protest!" he shouted.

ALL the nobles came to their feet. Lardon among them. Lardon was pointing at King.

"That man, that foreigner," he yelled, "has led the princess away from the tried and tested customs and laws of our fathers. He has bewitched her, has encouraged her to try to set aside our most precious possession. I cry protest against the voicing of the law and I cry protest against that man." He pointed at King.

A dozen voices were instantly crying protest. There was a babble of sound. It lasted for an instant. The commoners, the workers, the technicians, sitting in the vast bowl, looked in confusion at each other. They did not know what was going on. A law and a custom of centuries had been changed. That they, the common people, would get large benefits from this change had not yet occurred to them. They hadn't had time to think, yet. The nobles, led by Lardon, had either been forewarned of the changing of the law, or they thought faster. They knew what to do.

A *chad* was launched straight toward King.

A dozen of the deadly balls leaped toward Avena.

More of the *chad* whirled angrily over the nobles who controlled them but were not launched at the princess or at King. Either they were being held in reserve or the hunters who controlled them had not yet made up their minds what to do.

A shocked gasp went up from the assembled Akkar! Avena had changed the laws. The nobles had promptly rebelled. Seconds after the law had been made, they were destroying their ruler.

King came to his feet. He leaped down the tiers of seats, trying to reach the nobles. He had only seconds to live. If he could dodge the *chad*, reach Avena— "Damned foolishness!" he grunted. He didn't have a chance.

The balls were driving straight toward Avena. She did not move.

Ten feet away from her, ten feet away from King, the *chad* stopped in midair. They hung there, not moving. An instant before, they had been driving toward their target as fast as so many arrows. Now they were stopped, hanging motionless in the air.

A mocking smile was on Avena's face.

"Well," she spoke.

The nobles stared in consternation from her to the *chad*. Some of them fumbled with the jewels that controlled the deadly little balls.

"*Well!*" Avena spoke again. Now the ring of steel was in her voice.

Silence. The multitude stared.

"Who cries protest of my laws?" Avena demanded.

Not a voice answered.

"Then obey the laws that I have decreed. Now, out of my presence, all of you!"

LIKE a breaking milldam pouring out its waters in flood, the assembled Akkar ran from the bowl. Like mountain goats, some scrambled up the tiers, others scuttled out the side entrances. The nobles ran with the rest, seemed glad of the chance to run. Oddly their *chad* followed them now.

King stared in amazement at the spectacle.

Somewhere near him a voice chuckled. It was Kathor. "You…" King whispered.

The aged technician nodded. "We knew they would protest. We knew they would rebel."

"But—"

"Their *chad* failed to obey them? Naturally. You see, I and the workers under me repair and tune the *chad*. We simply changed the tuning so that all of the balls, without the knowledge of their users, were under the control of Avena. Thus when the nobles tried to attack her, and you, she simply stopped the flight of the *chad!*"

"Good Lord!" King gasped.

Avena was descending from the throne, coming toward them.

"Well, man from another world, what do you think now?" she questioned.

"I think you are very brave and very strong person," King answered. "And I am proud of you."

"Thank you."

"But—I am wondering."

"Yes?"

"Lardon and the nobles, they won't take this change lying down. You've got them whipped now, because they don't know what happened to their *chad*. But when they find out what happened, they'll be back to see us, and, unless I miss my guess, there will be trouble."

"Of course there will be trouble," the girl answered. "But there is always trouble. And we are not afraid, you and I...are we?"

"Maybe you're not," King answered. "But I sure as hell am..."

CHAPTER NINE

ODDLY, during the days that followed, the noble hunters of Akkan made no effort to resist the decree that had deprived them of most of their privileges. They could be seen going about the streets of the city directing the work of the clean-up squads, supervising the repair of the buildings. It was a long job they had ahead of them. Centuries of neglect could not be repaired in a few days. Months—years—would be needed. But eventually Akka would be restored to its former beauty.

"At least they can look forward to steady employment," King said to Avena, as they watched one of the groups moving blocks of stone.

Silently she assented. These days she was mostly given to silences. Watching her surreptitiously, King could not begin to understand her. He knew that in the past she had been a deadly huntress of humans, the leader of the hunting caste of Akkan. In a few words she had decreed the end of hunting forever, she had uprooted a whole social system, and instead of being a wasteful idler, had become a hard worker for the welfare of her people. She had made a tremendous change in the lives of the Akkar, and she, too, had changed. The silences were an indication of the change but the thoughts that moved in the back of that sleek head she kept strictly to herself. On one point she was adamant. She would not go back into the forests nor would she permit King to go. He wanted to get back to his comrades, to tell them what had happened, to let them know they were free to come out of hiding, that no longer would they be hunted like wild animals through the game preserves. King could not tell Avena they existed and to all his suggestions that he go to the forests just to look around she returned a firm, "No."

"Why?" he questioned.

"I now hate the forests of the game preserves," she answered. "I hate them. I—I used to hunt there."

Only a psychiatrist could have provided a satisfactory explanation for her reaction, but she seemed to have decided that hunting was wrong and in consequence had no desire to go back to the hunting grounds and be reminded of the things she had done there in the past.

IF AVENA was silent, Kathor was bubbling over with jubilant talk. "Now," the aged technician was constantly saying. "Now we can make progress again. Now the long years, the long centuries of stagnation are finished. We can begin research—I have already made plans—into all the sciences. We can reopen the neglected schools. Possibly…" He looked slyly at King. "…we can go into your world and see for ourselves, meet your scientists, your wise men. By pooling the knowledge of two worlds, each world would gain much."

"Possibly," said King. "But in the meantime, are you sure these nobles are going to take their slap in the face lying down?"

"Of course. What else can they do? Avena has the whip hand over them and they are powerless." Kathor was quite emphatic but to King his certainty sounded like wishful thinking. He didn't like the looks of those hunters.

"Hmmm. Avena, of course, can stop the action of their *chad*. But at how great a distance is her control effective?"

"At how great a distance?" A sudden worried frown furrowed Kathor's forehead. "Why any *chad* within two hundred paces she can control at will. If her own *chad* is freshly charged, her control will be effective for at least three hundred paces. You don't think—"

"I'm not doing the thinking around here," King answered. "But if I were one of those former hunters I would go three hundred yards away from the princess and laugh at her. What would she do then?"

"Why—why—" the technician sputtered. "They haven't even discovered how she controls their *chad*. They haven't thought—"

"They haven't, eh? Where is Lardon?"

"Lardon? Lardon. Now that you mention it—"

"You haven't seen him since he tried to rebel!" King finished for him. "And neither have I."

"I'll institute a search immediately," Kathor promised. Like an agitated rabbit, he went hopping away.

King turned to Avena. "You, my lovely lady, are sitting on top of a powder keg."

"I am not afraid," she answered. "In Akkan, we believe that no one dies but once."

"We have the same saying in my world," King answered. "But we put another twist on it. You may only die once but when you do die you're dead a helluva long time."

SINCE she would not do it, King took precautions. He very carefully inspected her guards, and without her knowledge set special guards at night. Kathor helping, he instituted a careful system designed to catch sneaking killers trying to approach in the dark. In the meantime, Lardon remained missing, nor could Kathor uncover any trace of him.

Then, entering his rooms late one night, King discovered what had happened to Lardon.

There was a dead man, lying naked and face down on the floor. A neat round hole, the work of a *chad*, had been burned between his shoulder blades. King dropped to his knees, turned the man over, and recoiled.

The man was not an Akkar. He was an American. He was Hillson, Sorenson's prize assistant.

A Yank, from Sorenson's hideaway, dead in King's rooms in the palace of Avena.

Lying beside him was a note. It was written in English!

"We have your friends who were hiding in the caverns. As proof that we have them, we offer this man. A knife in the throat of the Princess Avena will win for you and for them free passage back to your world. Fail us in this and one by one we will lay your friends before you, the girl last. Choose!"

The note was signed "Akbad."

Lardon had gone for Akbad. The ruler of the Temple of Forbidden Delight had come here, to Akkan, to direct the revolt of the nobles! Somehow the presence of the Americans had been discovered. Akbad was using them as a lever to force King to strike at Avena. And Hillson, whose heart and soul had been wrapped up in electro-dynamics; Hillson, with his penchant for tinkering and his mechanical mind, lay dead in King's room.

A KNIFE in Avena's throat or your friends die one by one! Leda. Leda of the clear blue eyes and the tiny fringe of freckles on her nose. Leda will die last. King had a vision of finding her in his room. Leda, with a hole burned through her. He sickened as revulsion shot through him. He had another vision, of a knife driving into the white throat of Avena, life ebbing from her in a spurting stream of red, and the sickness deepened.

"Lord!" he groaned. "Why don't I just commit suicide and have it over with?"

Avena—or Leda and the Americans! He did not in the least doubt that Akbad would carry out his threat. Either Avena died by King's hand or one by one corpses would be laid on his doorstep. Akbad had shrewdly selected the one person who could get to her.

The creak of the opening door came to his ears. The note still in his fingers, he leaped to his feet. The door opened.

Avena and Kathor entered. They looked at King, then their eyes centered on the body on the floor.

"What is this?" Kathor questioned.

"I found him here when I came in," King answered.

"Did you kill him? No, I see you didn't." Examining the body, Kathor had already discovered the mark of the *chad*. Almost instantly he made another discovery, one that startled him even more than the body himself. "Hello! This man is no Akkar! He—he—" Kathor looked at King.

"So I had discovered," King said.

"But how would an American, how would one of your race, get here?"

"Probably the same way I got here—through Akbad's genial hospitality."

"Yes, of course." Kathor turned perplexed eyes toward Avena. "We have forgotten about Akbad. Something must be done—"

Avena nodded. "I agree that something must be done about Akbad. But at the moment I am more concerned about—" She looked at King.

He thrust the note into his pocket. "You mean…they are trying to kill me? I don't think so. If they had wanted to kill me, they would have killed me and that would have been the end of it. As to the mystery of this man, I don't know a thing, except that I found him here. As to who killed him, or why, or how he got here—" He shrugged. "I was just going to call you when you entered." His eyes passed quickly over her throat.

Perplexed, Avena looked at him. She didn't dispute what he had said but she didn't exactly seem to believe him either. The doubt in her mind was mirrored on her face. "Kathor and I had come to talk," she said. "This—this rather gives me something else to think about. Come, Kathor."

Turning, she left the room. The aged technician bobbed after her.

A FEW minutes later slaves entered and removed the body from the floor. King made no objection. Opening the door, he discovered that extra palace guards had been posted in the corridor outside his room.

Had they been placed there to protect him from what Avena thought was an assassination attempt, or had they been assigned to keep him under close watch?

"Damn!" he said. In his mind was a single thought: What the hell was he going to do? A glitter on the table in the room caught his eyes. A dagger with a six-inch blade that was razor-sharp and needlepointed lay there. Left for him to use! For a long time he stared at the knife. Then he picked it up, thrust it into his pocket. A grim look settled on his face.

King's preparations were swiftly made. He made a roll out of a small rug, placed it in his bed. Anyone glancing into the room would think that he was safely asleep, he hoped! His more fervent hope was that no one would look for him. He went to the window, gently shoved the heavy pane aside. A tough clinging vine similar to ivy had found the wall to its liking. Its knotted, winding branches were an inch thick. King gently tested them. Like a slowly moving shadow he went down the wall.

Half an hour later he was in Lardon's bedroom.

"Damn!" he said.

Lardon was absent. King had hoped the bull-necked noble would have returned. If he could find Lardon—well, there were some questions he wanted to ask, questions that Lardon might be able to answer.

"What now?" he half-whispered to himself.

Logically, there was only one thing to do—search until he had found another noble. The probability was that others beside Lardon would be able to answer his questions. He turned to the door, started to leave, then stopped. Stealthy footsteps were audible in the hall outside. Back against the wall, King crouched in the shadows, waiting. The barely burning glow light provided the only illumination in the room. The door opened an inch. King held his breath.

SOMEONE out there in the hall was peering intently into the room. A thief, King wondered. Or an assassin?

It might be either. Lardon was rich enough and displayed his wealth openly enough to attract the attention of all the thieves in Akka. He was also ruthless enough to have made many enemies. King waited. The door opened another inch, then was shoved all the way open. Lardon entered the room.

He went directly to a heavy metal chest, stooped over it, and began to fumble with the lock. No *chad* floated over him.

King's voice in his ear sent a gasping wheeze from his throat.

"If you move, I'll have this knife in your back."

"What? Who—what—"

"Shut up…"

"Uh!"

The needlepoint of the blade pricked him in the back. "What—who are you?"

"Turn around and look."

Lardon turned slowly. A grimace passed over his face when he saw King.

"You…" he whispered.

"Yes."

"What—what do you want?"

"I want you to take me to the Americans that Akbad is holding prisoner."

"What?"

"You heard me…"

"But—I can't do that. I mean, I don't know what you're talking about. I don't know anything about any prisoners. Who—who is Akbad?"

"I heard you the first time," King said.

"But I don't—"

"Shut up! Either you take me to them or—"

Lardon was still on his knees. Halfway turned around, he was looking up. The knifepoint went through the robe he was wearing, went into his flesh.

"Don't—don't—don't!"

"Either take me where I want to go or—" Projecting an inch beyond his fingers in the deadly grip of the knife fighter, the flick of King's wrist sent the blade of the knife through the air a fraction of an inch from Lardon's throat.

"Don't—" he gulped.

"Either or else."

"I'll take you, I'll take you, I'll take…" Lardon spoke so rapidly that the words ran together. He rose to his feet.

WITH King following a step behind him, he led the way out of the room. "If you are tempted to try to escape," King said, "remember I'll have this knife between your ribs before you can take a second step. I can also do a very nice job of throwing it," he added grimly.

"I'll take you to them," Lardon promised.

"Take me so we don't get caught," King cautioned. "If you lead me into a trap and some of your friends jump me, I'll get you before they get me."

From his start, King guessed that Lardon had been planning exactly that. "I'll take you by a secret path," he said. And because there was a knife at his back, he kept his promise, but before he reached the place where the Americans were held, there were many times when King thought the Akkar was deliberately leading him on a wild goose chase.

The Americans were not held in a building in the city, as King had thought they would be. Nor were they in the surrounding forest, although Lardon started in that direction. The path he eventually took led downward into a labyrinth of caves so extensive they seemed to extend for miles. Using an adaptation of the glow lamps as a flashlight to illuminate their way, Lardon moved cautiously through the caverns. He was scared, though it was impossible to tell whether the source of his fear lay in the knife held at his back, in the possibility that Akbad might discover them, or in something else. Nervously Lardon looked over his shoulder, his eyes darting in every direction. Sweat dripped from his face.

"Sweat, damn you," King said. "If you're tricking me, you won't sweat long."

"I'm not tricking you," the Akkar protested. "The prisoners are held not far ahead. Be a little more careful with that knife."

"What about the guards?"

"There are no guards. I—we—the possibility of rescue never occurred to us so we did not think it necessary to place guards over them."

"Good," King grunted.

"We are there," Lardon said. "Here is the door of the room where they are held. See…I did not trick you."

A GRILL of heavy iron bars was the door. It was set in massive iron hinges bolted against the stone. Thick bars of iron crossed the front of the grill, effectively shutting it. The whole device was primitive in the extreme but it was ingeniously constructed so that the prisoner held behind those bars had no chance of escaping by his own efforts.

And there was someone behind the bars! King caught a glimpse of movement, as of someone drawing back out of sight, when he came up. Lardon turned the light from his torch into the cell. Then, from behind the iron grill, a voice drawled.

"Well I'll be damned! If it isn't Sandy King."

Cal Carson's voice. A voice King would know anywhere.

"Cal…are you and the others all there? Are you all right?"

"We're all right," Carson answered. "And all of us are here except Hillson. They took him away and he didn't come back. I don't know what happened to him."

"I know," King gritted. He shoved the bars out of their niches. They came crowding out to greet him with exclamations of astonishment. Leda and James Sorenson, her father looking as though he had aged years since King saw him last; Rogers, Sin Yul, the technicians he had met working in Sorenson's laboratory.

"King!"

"We're glad you turned up, old man."

"What the hell happened to you?"

"Glad to see you alive, sir. Make leave to guess they got you knocked in head by now." This was Sin Yul speaking. "How you find us boss?"

"Lardon here was kind enough to guide me," King grinned, nodding toward the Akkar. "As to anything else you want to know, it will have to wait. Come on. We've got to get away from here."

"What are you going to do with me?" Lardon protested.

"We'll take you with us. Avena will know what to do with you."

"Avena! If you turn me over to her, she will have me killed."

"I think not," King answered. "You may be a rat but you've earned your life and I think she'll let you keep it.

Come on. Lead us out of here, Lardon. I want to take these people to Avena immediately."

At a trot, Lardon started to lead them out of the caverns. King followed close behind him. He had no intention of trusting the Akkar out of reach of his knife, not until they were safely back in the city. As they hurried along, he told the story of what had happened to him.

"You mean Avena had announced the end of the hunting in Akkan?" Sorenson questioned incredulously.

"Yes."

"I can scarcely believe it. After all, for her to renounce hunting would require changing her whole nature. It would be easier for the leopard to change its spots than for the ruler of Akkan to change the hunting customs of herself and her people."

"That's what she did," King insisted.

"That may be," Sorenson stubbornly said. "But I have been living in fear of her and of her nobles for too many years to accept that idea easily. I'll believe it when I see it."

"You'll see it soon enough," King answered. "We have been misjudging her. She was a huntress because hunting was the custom of her people and no one had ever told her it was wrong. Good Lord, what's that?"

ALMOST running over Lardon, he slid to a halt. Ahead of them, dancing in the darkness of the large cavern through which they were passing, was a glowing *chad*. It was coming slowly toward them.

"Back!" King ordered.

Before he could move, he saw, out of the corner of his eyes, a *chad* appear behind them. It seemingly dropped from up above. On their right was a wall. To the left was the darkness of a large cavern.

Dropping from somewhere above them, like snowflakes in a sudden storm, were dozens of the glowing balls. Lardon suddenly gibbered in fear. Carson cursed. Leda gasped. King stood without moving. A sloping ledge coming down the wall on their right provided a passage from somewhere up above down to their level. Akkar were descending the ledge.

It was these Akkar who controlled the *chad*. They had spotted the Americans passing below, and had trapped them.

CHAPTER TEN

A FILE of robe-clad Akkar came swiftly down the ledge. Moving with the precision of a well-trained infantry drill team, they surrounded the Americans, hemmed them against the wall, the glowing *chad* darting overhead.

King looked at Lardon. "If ever I get out of here alive, you had better start running and never stop."

In his mind was the thought that Lardon had led them into a trap, that he had taken them along a route where Akbad would be certain to discover them. He turned to face the leader of the group that had caught them.

The leader wasn't Akbad. It was Avena. Kathor was with her. They came down the ledge, walked toward him. The light of the glowing *chad* clearly revealed Avena's face. Marble-white, it was stone hard. No trace of any emotion showed on it. Her gaze went from King to the group with him, rested for a moment on Lardon, then returned to King.

"Well?" she said.

"Where did you come from?"

"I sent Kathor to your quarters to talk to you. When he reported you were missing, I ordered a search. One of my men reported he had seen you and someone else slipping into the caverns. We came here looking for you."

"I see."

"What do you have to say for yourself?"

"Is it necessary that I say anything?"

"I think you had better say something," Avena answered, and her voice was as cold as a wind blowing over glacial ice. "I find you here with a man who is my deadly enemy, with Lardon, who tried to revolt against my laws. I also find you with a group of your own people, a group that I never knew existed. The appearance is that you are conspiring against me."

The words were ice cold. King could not question the remorseless logic in them. From her viewpoint, it looked as if he might be conspiring against her!

He shrugged. "Do you believe that?"

"What I believe is of no importance. What are you doing with Lardon?"

"Ask Lardon," King answered.

"I'm asking you."

KING was silent. What could he say? Could he tell her that he had forced Lardon at the point of a knife to guide him to the Americans?

"Who are these people?" She pointed at the Americans.

"Friends of mine."

"What are they doing here? How did they get here?"

"That's a question I would like to have answered myself," King said. "They were brought here. But how they were discovered in the first place—" Ever since he had learned the Yanks had been captured and were being held as prisoners, this question had been in the back of his mind: How had they been caught in the first place? How had Akbad learned their hiding place?

"Who brought them here?"

King shrugged.

"Enough of this!" Her voice was zero cold. "If you have an explanation, I am willing to listen. If not—"

The deadly billiard balls danced madly at her implied threat. King knew she meant what she said. Deep within him admiration surged. He had lived a hard life among hard people and he could understand and appreciate hardness when he met it. She was hard, as hard as steel, when the situation demanded it. And she had courage, the courage to be ruthless. He grinned.

"When you put your foot down, you really put it down, don't you? Okay, Avena, if you must know why Lardon is here—he came at my urgent invitation. And I came because of these." He handed her the knife and the threatening note.

The knife she could understand, the note, written in English, she could not understand. As he translated it for her and as the meaning reached her mind, all traces of color left her cheeks.

"King! Either you killed me or he killed your friends!"

"Something like that."

"But why didn't you come to me?"

"And have Akbad deliver these people to me one by one? Almost certainly he has spies around you. He would learn that I had told you of his threat."

"But if you had come to me I could have given you help in finding and rescuing them. You might have been killed, trying to save them without help."

King laughed. "We are not afraid of death, you and I. Remember, Avena, when you said that?"

She shivered, shook her head. "I would rather not be reminded. I did not mean—"

THE hard, brittle shell with which she surrounded herself had been broken. For a moment the real person underneath the shell showed through, a very badly frightened, badly scared girl who was putting up a front.

"What—what are we going to do?"

"Goodness gracious!" King drawled. "Does that question mean you've decided I'm to run the show from now on?"

"Well—"

"Yes or no."

"Yes," she said breathlessly. "You are 'running the show.' What are we going to do?"

"The first thing—get the hell out of here while we can. The second thing—find Akbad. Lardon, here, may be able to help us in that."

"I don't know a thing," Lardon said hastily. "Akbad—"

"Didn't exactly trust you, eh?" Carson then shot a hard glance at King. "Well...what is it, Cal?"

"I want to talk to you, Sandy," the ex-sergeant said.

"Go on and talk."

"I mean alone."

"Oh... Okay." He followed Carson away from the group. "What have you got on your mind, Cal?"

"I think I know how we were captured."

"Really? Then make with the information. How did they manage to catch all of you?"

"We were in the cave and we didn't know anybody was within miles of us," Carson answered. "Bingo! These gorillas popped up all around us. We didn't have a chance. They seemed to know every entrance, every hiding place in the joint."

"Yes?"

"It means somebody told them where we were and how to get there. Their information was perfect. They knew exactly where we were and how to go to get to us."

"Damn! Who—"

"Sin Yul…"

"Sin Yul?"

Carson nodded doggedly. "I think so. He was missing a long time before we were captured. Later, after they had caught us, those gorillas came dragging him in as if they had found him hiding someplace. I don't think they found him hiding. I think he went to them and told them where we were. After they had caught us, I think they planted him back on us so as a spy."

"BUT that doesn't seem possible," King protested. "Sin Yul would have no motive for betraying you. He wouldn't gain anything by it."

"The hell he wouldn't! I think he went to the city on an exploring expedition of his own, and got caught. When he discovered which way the wind was blowing, he told Akbad where we were. He would gain something by turning us in. He would get to be on what he thought would be the winning side. And that's kind of important, Sandy, to be on the winning side."

Carson's reasoning seemed logical enough. "Damn him, anyhow…" King said. "I'll shake the truth out of him. Sin Yul!" he called out. "Come here…"

There was no answer.

"Where the hell is he? He was here when I opened that door and turned you loose, Sin Yul!"

A quick search revealed that Sin Yul was missing. King stared at Carson. "That tears it," he said. "That dirty such-and-such. If he's missing, there can be only one meaning—that he has gone to Akbad! Come on. Let's get out of here."

As if in answer, from somewhere in the darkness overhead there came a burst of laughter. A faraway voice whispered, "You may find that easier to say than to do, Captain King, much easier to say than to do."

Akbad's voice! Akbad's faraway whisper, coming through the medium of a *chad,* the whisper as they had first heard it in the ruined Dak bungalow outside the temple of Forbidden Delight, in Upper Burma.

Simultaneously from somewhere up above there came a scream as a sentinel that Avena had left behind to serve as a lookout found sudden death striking him. A *chad* streaked with red light leaped into sight in the darkness overhead. An object hurtled down through the darkness to strike with a heavy thud on the floor—the luckless sentinel.

Instantly there leaped out from the shelf where the sentry had been hiding—dozens of glowing billiard balls! Like falling stars they dropped downward toward the group below.

Akbad had caught Avena and her entire party in a deadly trap. Avena and Kathor, many of the technicians who had supported the change in the laws of Akkan, part of the loyal palace guard, he had caught them all. The *chad* hurtling downward showed what he intended to do.

"Stop those *chad!*" King barked.

FROM the floor he scooped up the knife that he had given to Avena and which she had dropped. The gesture was instinctive. He could not fight one of those glowing billiard balls with a knife. Avena would have to stop them. She had stopped the *chad* when the nobles had attempted to rebel. She would stop them again.

King saw the look of concentration deepen on her face as the mental impulses flowed out through the *chad* that she controlled.

"Stop!" he seemed to hear her say. "I order you to stop."

The dropping *chad* faltered in their flight, hesitated for an instant, then continued coming down. They were moving slower now, but they were still moving.

Avena looked at King. Startled surprise was on her face. "I can't—control them!" she whispered.

"You can't!"

"No."

"They have discovered the changes we made in the *chad!*" Kathor gasped. "They have changed them so that Avena no longer has control over them. Fight!"

Although King had not thought about it until that moment, it was logical that a people who had developed a weapon such as the *chad*, who used it for hunting and for fighting, would also have developed a method of defense against it. Weapons and defenses had developed that way on Earth. The shield had been developed as a defense against the bow, the sword, and the spear. Steel mail was still a later method of protection. When the machine gun was invented, trench warfare had appeared as a countermeasure. When the tank appeared on the scene, the mobile antitank gun had put in an appearance.

What did the Akkar use to defend themselves against the *chad?*

King saw what they used. *Chad!*

The weapon was its own defense. Sword against sword, bow against bow, rifle against rifle, cannon against cannon, *chad* against *chad.* As Kathor, Avena, her guards and Kathor's trusted technicians went into action; the vast cavern was instantly filled with dozens of fiercely contested duels. The loyal guard formed a solid ring around Avena. In front of them, over them, behind them, their own *chad* darted. Like fierce duelists armed with blobs of ball lightning instead of swords, they thrust and counterthrust at each other. The *chad* darting toward a guard was met and turned aside. Or was not met and turned aside. In which case the *chad* vanished to reappear a moment later red-filmed above the body of the falling guard. King saw three of the guards go down, saw Kathor fumbling with a left arm that no longer existed, saw Avena narrowly avert a *chad* charging at her, and knew that this battle could have but one end.

"Retreat!" he yelled.

AVENA heard and understood him. At her order the guards began a fighting retreat toward the dark tunnel at the far end of the cavern. Once there, they would have a fighting chance. But first they had to get there.

"Carson. Rogers. Two others!"

The Americans standing to one side had taken no part in the fight as yet. Probably because they did not represent a source of danger, the *chad* had not attacked them. Once Avena and her followers had gone down, the unarmed Americans would present no problem. So, for the present, Akbad left them alone.

"What is it, Sandy?"

"The rest of you get out of here the best way you can. You four come with me."

With Carson and the other three at his heels he slid along the wall until he came to the sloping edge.

"We going up, Sandy?" Carson questioned.

"We are," King answered.

"Wish I had me a Tommy-gun."

"So do I," King said. "But all I've got is a knife and all you've got is your fists. They're not enough but they're all we've got. If we can distract that bunch up above for a few minutes, Avena will have a chance to get away."

"Yeah."

"Keep close to the wall and pray they're too busy to notice us."

Like shadows, King and the four men went up the ledge. It was a rough natural slope, the product of some mountain convulsion of the long past. The footing was rough but the cover was good. King reached the top.

Akbad was readily visible. Leaning eagerly over the ledge, he was directing the activities of his *chad* fighting down below. With him was—Sin Yul.

"That rat!" King grated. "As soon as we turned him loose he ran straight to Akbad and told him where we were. That's how he located us so damned easily."

From the sloping ledge, King leaped up to the shelf. Akbad saw the movement.

"Look out!" he yelled.

Knife in hand, King dived toward him. Akbad ducked away. Simultaneously a noble looking up just in time to see what was happening butted his head into King's stomach. The move was as unexpected as it was disastrous. All the air knocked out of him. King fell heavily. His head struck the wall behind the shelf. He was knocked instantly unconscious.

King was out only a few seconds. As consciousness slowly returned, he found Sin Yul bending over him. Sin Yul was talking too fast to be understood.

DOWN on the shelf a hell of a fracas was going on. A knot of nobles surrounded something. One of the nobles suddenly lifted into the air. Arms and legs whirling, he was thrown over the edge of the shelf, went soaring downward like some vast ungainly bird.

"Give 'em hell, Cal!" King croaked. It was Carson and the other two Yanks down there in the knot of nobles. Swinging fists, feet, kicking, slugging, they were putting up a good fight. It was a fight that could have but one end. A gleaming *chad* darted up from below.

"Look out," King croaked. "They're calling back their dogs." He tried to get to his feet. There was no strength in his legs. "Huh? What's that?"

Sin Yul had forced himself into King's vision. "What's that you said?"

"You going to die, Yank!" Sin Yul repeated.

King considered this. It did not seem at all remarkable to him. "So what?" he said. "So what if I don't care?"

"You care plenty," Sin Yul shrieked. "You think me Burmese? Me no Burmese. Me Japanese!"

"Huh?" King heard the words but they didn't seem to make sense.

"High command hear stories of this land," Sin Yul shouted. He was apparently determined that King would pay attention to him. "Send me to investigate. You hire as guide. Not know this very place me trying to reach. Hah! Smart Yank fooled by Japanese."

"Well...I'm damned," King said. "A Japanese spy..." Sin Yul's words had finally penetrated to his consciousness.

"Me get secret of glass airship, secret of *chad*, take back to Japan," Sin Yul gloated. "Japan use to fight another war. This time Yankees don't win. How you like that, huh?"

King was silent. Shocked comprehension had numbed his brain. The war lords of Japan, with the secret of the *chad*, the secret of the glass bubbles that floated so easily. He could easily imagine what that meant, Japanese industry would build those deadly weapons in secret, ferret out the design, improve on it. Pearl Harbor would happen all over again. Pearl Harbor on a bigger, vastly more destructive scale.

"How you like that, huh?" Sin Yul exulted.

"I don't like it," King said.

"Nothing you can do about it, Yankee. You die now. See *chad*. Me got *chad*. See *chad* coming, Yankee."

ENJOYING his moment of triumph, Sin Yul sent the *chad* toward King. An inch at a time it moved closer. King stared at it, at the grinning face behind it. Sin Yul had certainly fooled him.

"See *chad* coming, Yank!"

"See knife coming, Jap!"

With all his strength, King struck upward. The knife was buried to its hilt in Sin Yul's chest.

A look of horrified astonishment spread over his face. He clutched at the knife handle, staggered, fell, and did not get up. His uncontrolled *chad* hung motionless.

"Give 'em hell, Cal!" King screamed, leaping to his feet.

A battle was going on there on the shelf where Carson and the three Yanks fought against desperate odds. Like

King, Carson had had extensive commando training, and with that type of experience he had learned just about everything there was to know about rough and tumble fighting. But commando training or not, there could be only one end to this fight. King knew the end, knew it was close when one of the Americans screamed as a *chad* burned its way through him.

"Destroy them!" Akbad was yelling.

King stumbled toward the group.

It seemed to dissolve in front of him, dissolve in a flare of milky billiard balls that moved so rapidly they looked like shooting stars. At the same instant, Akbad stopped yelling. Abruptly the nobles lost all interest in the fight and began to run. Stupefied, King stared at them, wondering what had caused their sudden flight. He saw the reason. A dozen of her guards behind her, Avena came up the ledge. The *chad* that had attacked the nobles came from this group. She saw King.

"Are you all right?"

"I'm alive," he said. "I'm alive."

From the tangle of bodies on the rough floor of the ledge, Carson rose to his feet. "So am I, Sandy," he said. "And am I surprised…"

One Yank was dead. A second could barely walk. A *chad* had grazed his leg, shearing a hole through the flesh. Carson, Rogers, were badly battered, but alive.

King surveyed the scene. "Anyhow, Akbad has retreated. Now I think we had better get the hell out of here ourselves."

Avena nodded agreement. "We must get out and rally all my people. They will fight on my side in this battle. I know they will."

"Then come on," King said. "And thanks for charging up this ledge."

"You're welcome," she smiled.

CHAPTER ELEVEN

THREE hours later they were still in the caverns, and facing one grim fact: they were not going to get out, not without a battle against hopeless odds.

Every exit was guarded by Akbad's nobles. Every time they had come to an exit they had discovered a cleverly laid ambush set for them.

"Sandy, it looks like we're destined to stay here," Cal Carson said.

"Looks that way," King admitted. "But anyhow they're not coming in after us. And if they do come in, they'll not only have a hell of a time finding us in this labyrinth but they'll have to dodge some ambushes of ours." He turned to Avena. "Do you think they'll come in after us?"

"No," she said. "Akbad will not quite dare. He controls many of the nobles but many others are only half-hearted in their rebellion. He doesn't dare trust the half-hearted ones. They might find me and betray him. So he will make them guard the exits. Meanwhile, he will try to plan some way to destroy us."

"Terrific. Such as?"

"I don't know. But whatever he does, must be done quickly, before the people learn what he is attempting and come to my rescue."

"Do you think they will come?"

"I know it. They will support my new laws because the laws benefit them. I think they have caught something of the vision I had, that Kathor had, of a new and glorious

Akkan, of peace and progress and honest work, of a marching forward in the way that our ancestors did before we got off the track. Yes, they will support me. The workers, the technicians, the scientists, because I have given them something to live for…"

She seemed very sure.

In the world outside the caverns, dawn was breaking. Looking out, they could see the streaks of day beginning to appear. King saw something else.

"Maybe that's your people coming now," he said, pointing.

Out there beyond the cave he had caught a glimpse of movement. The movement continued. In a few minutes it had resolved itself into vast number of Akkar—all moving toward the cave.

"They're coming!" Avena thrilled. "They're coming. I told you they would come."

"By gad, you're right!" King said. The sight of the Akkar coming to the caverns to rescue their princess sent a surge of emotion through him. They were all right, those Akkar, once they learned the way. Or at least the common people, the workers, the technicians, were all right. He still had his doubts about the nobles, but seeing the approaching throng he could no longer doubt that the great multitude was back of their ruler, coming to save her.

BACK in the darkness of the cavern a sentry on guard cried a sharp challenge. "Someone comes!" he called out.

"Bring him here," Avena ordered.

The guard led the Akkar forward. He was panting, gasping for breath, so near exhaustion that he could barely stand. He threw himself on the ground before Avena.

"My Princess! I knew he lied. I came. I hunted for you. I have run and run—"

"What's this?" Avena sharply questioned.

The Akkar fought for breath to continue. "Akbad! Lardon!" he whispered. "Akbad came to us. He said that the real Princess Avena was dead, that this magician from Earth…" He pointed to King. "…had killed her. Akbad said that this magician had put another princess in your place, a spurious, false princess, that it was this false princess who had announced the changing of the laws. Akbad told us that he and the nobles had trapped the magician and a number of other magicians in the caverns and—and—" He ran out of breath.

Avena gasped. King saw the lines of fear dig into her face. There was silence in the cave, complete silence.

"But that isn't true," Avena protested.

"I knew it wasn't true and I came to tell you," the messenger answered. "But everyone else believes it is true and—"

"And what?"

"They come to help Akbad hunt the magician and the false princess in the caverns, they come to destroy you."

As though his strength had run out, the messenger slid down to the ground. The wheeze of his panting lungs as he fought for breath was the only sound.

King looked at Avena. "So *that's* why they're coming," he said. "To hunt us down—"

Her soul was in her eyes. "I'm sorry," she said.

He patted her on the shoulder. "That's all right. We've done the best we could. Now—"

"Now we are going to do something else!"

He stared at her. "What do you mean?"

"I mean—Akbad hasn't won yet. There is still one course I can take. And I am going to take it. But first—" She hesitated, looked at King, looked from him to the Americans, looked back at him. "No, it would not be right. It would not be fair. Guards!"

Her guards snapped to attention.

"Hold this entrance. Let no one enter."

"Yes, Princess."

She looked at King. "You and your friends come with me."

"But what are you going to do?"

"Come. I'll show you. I know a trick that Akbad has forgotten."

FOUR of her guards and the Americans went with her. Moving at a trot, she turned back into the caverns. Without explaining, scarcely looking back, she went deeper and deeper into the caves until she was at least a mile underground. The glowing *chad* in front of her dimly lighted the way. They came to a place where the natural cave had been enlarged, where a tunnel had been dug ages past, they came to an iron grill that was a door. Her attendants swiftly removed the bars.

"Come on," she said, without hesitation.

King and the Americans followed her into a round chamber from which there was no exit. A split second too late King realized there was no way out except the way they had entered. "Hey—" he yelled, turning.

Clanging, the guards swung the grill shut. Avena was on the side away from the Americans. King stared at her.

"I am going back," she said. "To challenge Akbad to the Duel of the Ruler."

"Duel of the Ruler?"

"Yes. That is the privilege of the ruler of Akkan. When the laws are disputed or when anyone rebels, the ruler may challenge to the duel. Armed each with a *chad,* they fight in the arena. If the ruler wins, the laws are upheld. If the rebel wins, naturally the law is changed."

"But—you can't mean it!"

"I do mean it!"

"You are going to fight Akbad?"

"Yes."

"But— He won't fight you."

"If he refuses, even his own nobles will turn against him. Remember, they do not all of them support him wholeheartedly. If he refuses to meet me in the Duel of the Rulers, they will destroy him without mercy. That is our custom and the custom is stronger than Akbad. Yes, he will fight me. He will have no choice."

"But you can't do it. It's senseless. A custom like that could only be in effect when a man is on the throne. You're a woman—"

"Am I a coward because of that?"

"No. But— Dammit, Avena, if this is the only way out, let me fight the duel for you."

LIGHTS glistened in her eyes. "No," she said firmly. "This is my fight. I may not let another fight in my place."

King gave up. In the face of her determination, arguments were useless. "But why did you bring us here?" he demanded. "Why did you lock us up while you go back to fight a duel?"

"Because I am sorry," she said.

"Sorry? For what?"

"Sorry for some of the things I did when I was the Huntress of Akkan. I hunted your people. Because I am sorry for that, I am making certain that you and your friends are safe even—even if I lose to Akbad. And if I should lose, you and your friends would go back into the game preserves to furnish sport for Akbad and his nobles."

"I still don't understand," King protested. "Why have you locked us in here?"

"You will understand in a moment," she said. "Can't you feel it taking hold of you already? I can feel it out here."

"Feel what?"

"The blowing of the wind."

"What?" There was incredulous amazement in King's voice. As he spoke he realized he was feeling an invisible wind. Moving through every atom of his being, it was growing stronger every second.

"It is the Earth current," Avena said. "In this spot it flows back to your world. It will take you back. And now, Sandy King, good luck and goodbye. And—"

The current tugged at him, tugged again and again, tugged stronger and stronger. He grabbed the bars, tried to hold on, tried to fight. A little by a little his grip failed. He felt the current pick him up, carry him, lift him.

Her heart in her eyes, Avena smiled at him. And smiling, vanished.

CONSCIOUSNESS returned in the prickling of ten thousand tiny needles. King sat up, opened his eyes. He was on the side of a mountain in a small ruined temple that had been hollowed out of the edge of a cliff. A mile away across a gorge was—the warty toad that was the Temple of Forbidden Delight.

Burma! Upper Burma, Earth.

Across from him Carson was dazedly getting to his feet, Sorenson, Leda, Rogers. He noticed that Rogers was trying to help Leda and she was trying to help him. Once this would have meant something to him, but no longer. The others were there, the fliers from Sorenson's hidden laboratory. All there. All of them.

Avena had kept her promise.

King still held the knife in his hands. He looked across the gorge, to that squat temple in the mountain. He started toward it.

"Sandy! Sandy!" This was Carson calling. Carson running after him.

"Take them back to civilization, Cal. Take them wherever they want to go. That's your job." King nodded toward the Americans.

"And you?" Carson questioned.

King nodded across the gorge.

"So that's the way it is, Sandy?"

"That's the way it is."

"Good luck."

"Goodbye…"

King never quite realized how he got across the gorge, how he forded the roaring river at the bottom, how he climbed the steep road to the temple. There were guards at the temple, guards armed with cunning knives. They took one look at him, and fled. He entered. Somewhere deep within that granite mountain, he found the Earth current. It picked him up.

The pit? Yes, this was the pit. He climbed out of it. This was the place where he had met Leda, and this was the river where she had dived, this was the mountain. Over there—was Akkan. He walked toward the city. It had been morning when he left, morning of some day. It was dusk now. Night was near. He entered the city with the dusk. It was strangely deserted. The palace guards were gone. There weren't even any guards outside the chambers of the princess. Gently King opened the door.

Somewhere inside the dimly lit room he could hear someone sobbing. She was lying on a couch, sobbing. When his footsteps sounded, she looked up.

"King!"

"I came back, Avena. There was a fight?"

"It didn't come off."

"No?"

"Akbad refused the duel and his nobles tore him limb from limb."

"Oh."

He was glad to hear this. The fight had not come off. Akbad had turned coward. Yes, this was good to know. But somehow, Akbad and the doings of Akbad no longer seemed to be important.

"There's a balcony outside. I noticed it once."

"Yes."

She led the way. Outside there was the night, the soft night of Akkan, and a soft wind, and a million stars.

THE END